Prologue

HER PRESENCE was as tangible as the scent of damp earth on the wind shortly before the rain falls. He could feel her, smell her, taste her long before she came into sight. Once she would have been as welcome as a summer shower on a hot August day. But this year, like the rain, she was coming too late. Tanner's love for her had withered just like the crops in the field after the long summer's drought.

Now it was autumn. Time to burn the fields and turn the ashes over, allowing the scorched earth to restore itself for a new beginning next spring.

Tanner stood with one arm braced against the tractor, his hawklike eyes staring across the acres of farmland, waiting for Jodi to appear. He had no idea what to say to her; he only knew that he had to burn Jodi out of his heart, if there was ever to be room for a new love to grow.

At last she appeared, just a blur on the horizon, gradually taking shape as she drew closer. Jodi had arrived, with the same, sky-blue eyes and cloud of golden hair that had haunted him season after season.

She came to him with the strong, steady stride that had brought her across two continents with only a weathered, red pack hanging from her shoulders. Each step was taken without hesitation until she stood directly in front of Tanner, close enough for him to reach out and touch her, but he did not and knew she would not. She never reached out first.

"You're late."

"Better late than never," she said.

"I don't think so."

"You don't mean that," Jodi insisted, but a question mark had somehow appeared at the end.

"Yes, I do." The words came slowly, heavily, as if he had to reach deep inside to pull them out. Unable to maintain the icy facade face-to-face, Tanner turned away. "I waited. All summer long I waited. And you never came. Never called. Never even wrote. Not once."

"I'm sorry," she whispered.

Tanner forgot his plan to remain cool. He spun back around, the cold emotionless mask ripped away by an anger so livid, Jodi automatically stepped back, retreating from the heat of his wrath.

"You're sorry. That's all you can say? You're sorry. I spend months worrying about you, wondering if you're dead or alive, and all you can say is you're sorry?"

Her head bowed with guilt, she twisted her fingers together in a childish gesture. Her voice hushed, she repeated, "I'm sorry."

Tanner shook from head to toe with frustration. He wrapped his arms across his chest, holding himself in check. If he were to touch her now, it would be a toss-up whether he would kill her, make love to her or do both.

Jodi opened her mouth as if to speak and gulped air instead. Her voice weak, she tried again. "I started to

Always
JO MORRISON

Harlequin Books

TORONTO • NEW YORK • LONDON
AMSTERDAM • PARIS • SYDNEY • HAMBURG
STOCKHOLM • ATHENS • TOKYO • MILAN

To Penny, Kristine and my family,
with thanks for their help and support
To Newman with no regrets

Published August 1990

ISBN 0-373-25412-1

Lara's heart quickened at the very sight of him

She felt the dampness of her palms against the cold metal doorknob and realized suddenly that if she let Tanner in now, naked as she was beneath her robe, all her plans for the evening would be history.

Moving away from the peephole, she slid the safety chain on and opened the door a crack. "You can't come in yet," she said, "I'm not finished dressing."

"Sounds like a waste of time to me," Tanner murmured. "Why don't I just come in and get undressed? Then we can both be comfortable."

"No way," Lara replied. "I told you tonight is going to be different. If we're going to have a relationship, we're going to back up and do it right. That means a candlelight dinner and conversation, not just sex."

"Fine. I'm kind of hungry myself," Tanner agreed easily... too easily. "Let me in and I'll help you with zippers and things."

"Fat chance. I know you better than that, Tanner McNeil. As far as you're concerned, zippers only go one way, and it isn't up...."

Jo Morrison began writing her first novel, *Always*, shortly after separating from her husband of four years. She doesn't think it odd that someone on the verge of divorce would choose to write a *romance* novel. She's used her own experience to vividly recreate the emotions—the happiness and the sadness—inherent in every relationship. In addition, *Always* reflects Jo's belief that we have only failed if we haven't tried. "Love lost and love found," she says, "nothing hurts more, nothing feels better. In real life, I've experienced both once and hope to experience the latter again."

Enjoy *Always* and welcome this talented newcomer to Temptation. Look for the story of Hank and Susan Metcalf in Jo's next book—coming soon.

contact you several times, but . . ." She hesitated. ". . . I just didn't know what to say."

"How about, 'Hi, Tanner. I'm on my way home.' Or 'Hi, Tanner. I'm still alive, I'll just be a little late.' Is that so hard? Is that so much to ask?"

He wasn't surprised when she began to pace. Jodi had always been more comfortable when her feet were moving. "I just didn't want to fight over the phone, and you know I'm not good about writing letters. I tried, but . . ." Her voice trailed off helplessly.

"Just where the hell were you, Jodi? What was so important that you couldn't come back, even just for the summer?"

"I decided to go up North. Alaska. Canada. I hadn't been there yet. I've always come here for the summer, and it is too cold up there for my kind of traveling any other time."

Tanner's eyes followed her restless movements as he planned the moment to pounce. "That was more important than coming here? More important than being with me?" He saw Jodi wince at the challenge in his voice.

"You knew I'd be here eventually. Does it really make a difference what season?"

"Yes. It does make a difference. I've always missed you. Every harvest, when you weren't here to help. Every winter, when you weren't here to warm me. Every spring, when I just wanted someone to share the newness with. Now I know what it is like to miss you for all seasons. It was a hell of a long summer, Jodi."

"I know. I heard about the drought."

Tanner laughed without humor. "I wasn't talking about the weather. Yes, the drought was tough. I lost most of the crops, and what little was left cost me more to save than I'll ever be paid for."

He raised his hand as if to brush away the sweat that was only a memory. "The heat was hell, but it was nothing compared to what you put me through." He hesitated and then went on again, the anger replaced by a quiet resolve.

"I can't take it anymore, Jodi. If you're not here to stay, then maybe you had better just leave now."

"You don't mean that, Tanner," she said again.

"Yes, I do." Now he spoke in hardly more than a whisper, almost afraid to hear the words aloud. "I need someone who wants to be with me. Always. Not someone who comes and goes like the rain on the wind."

"I can't change, Tanner."

"You mean you won't."

"I mean I can't . . . and I won't."

"Not even for me? For us?"

"Especially not. We'd wind up hating each other."

Tanner's head jerked up sharply. "I would always love you."

"Then you'll have to love me while I'm here, after I'm gone and when I come back, because that's who I am, Tanner. That's what I am."

"Then somehow I'll just have to learn how to stop loving you, because I can't take this anymore."

Slowly he extended his hand, barely grazing her skin. With trembling fingers he caught the chain that circled her neck and followed it down to the locket hidden in the snug valley between her breasts. Lifting it gently, he cradled the gold piece in his palm, turning it so that the inscription on the back was visible.

If You Love Something, Set It Free. If It Comes Back to You, It Is Yours. And beneath that, in smaller script, Come Back. I Love You. Always. Tanner.

There was no need to read the words out loud. They both knew them by heart. He had given her the locket the first time she left him. Whenever it was time for them to say goodbye, he would hold it as he held it now, letting it speak for him, rather than risk saying the words that might drive her away forever.

"I always come back, Tanner."

"But only to leave me again. That doesn't make you mine." Taking a deep breath, he finally took the risk. "If you can't stay for good, don't stay at all, Jodi. I gave you your freedom. It's time you did the same for me."

"I have never tried to chain you," she protested.

"No, you've just asked me to wait, to put my life on hold, while you go in search of something I don't even understand. Well, I've been waiting for years now, Jodi, and those years of my life are as wasted as any man's in prison. I've got nothing to show for it but gray hairs and heartache."

"You could come with me. You enjoyed that summer after college. You've always said you did."

"Yes, I enjoyed it. It was a great experience. But it was the once-in-a-lifetime variety for me. This is my home, Jodi. I've no desire to become the next Arkansas Traveller."

For what seemed an endless time, they stared at each other, fresh out of words and too full of pain to speak, even if they'd had them.

A single tear began to slide down Tanner's cheek. Jodi brushed it away, ignoring the tears dampening her own face.

"I'll be back, Tanner."

"I won't be waiting this time," he warned her.

Clearly unable to stop herself, she asked, "Is there someone else?"

"Not yet, but there will be. I'm not going to spend another long, cold winter sleeping alone."

Jodi jerked her hand back as if he had struck her. Straightening her pack, she visibly gathered her pride and turned to face the dirt track snaking through the charred rice fields. Placing her left foot in front of her right, she began the hardest journey she would ever make.

Halfway through the field, she broke her own rule and turned around, walking backward so she could watch him as long as possible. As she disappeared, the wind carried her last words back to him.

"I always come back, Tanner McNeil. Always."

And then it began to rain.

1

"HE HAD THE BIGGEST..." Lara stopped abruptly as she realized that she had lost her audience to an attraction somewhere beyond her right shoulder. Turning slightly, she noticed a new arrival staggering his way to the bar.

Her table companions began to murmur at once, Lara's story entirely forgotten.

"I wondered if he would show up tonight."

"Question is, who's he going home with?"

"Well, just remember, if he asks for a volunteer, the line forms right behind me!"

"Fine, you can have him. Who wants a guy on the rebound?"

"Honey, at our age, we take them anyway we can get them."

"Excuse me," Lara said, finally interrupting her friends, "but would one of you mind telling me who it is we're discussing?"

"Sorry, but that's what you get for staying away so long. You miss out on all the juicy gossip."

"Susan!" Kelly exclaimed. "Be nice now, or she might decide to go back to the city." Patting Lara's arm reassuringly, she added, "Don't worry, we'll bring you up-to-date on who's doing what to whom."

"Thanks, I would appreciate that. Let's start with tall, drunk and handsome over there."

Both women eagerly jumped on what was apparently their latest favorite topic of conversation.

"That's Tanner McNeil. Don't you remember him, Lara?"

"I don't think so."

"Oh, of course she doesn't, Kelly. Lara was a couple of years behind us in school, and Tanner must have been at least two years ahead."

"Oh, that's right. I keep forgetting she's just a baby."

Lara grinned. "Twenty-eight is hardly a baby, Kel."

"It is to anyone over thirty. Take my word for it."

"Oh, don't pay any attention to her, Lara. She just turned thirty three weeks ago and hasn't gotten over the shock yet." Susan scoffed with the superiority of someone who had been thirty for at least six months.

"Well, would you two old ladies mind telling me why Tanner McNeil is here, drunk and on the rebound?"

"Careful," Susan warned, "or we may decide not to introduce you to Morristown's most recent eligible bachelor."

"Oh, is he getting divorced?" Lara looked again at the man who was now propping up the bar, automatically taking interest in a prospective client and fellow survivor.

"Well, not exactly," Susan hedged. "I mean he and Jodi were never really married."

Lara's mouth fell open as she turned back to her friend. "You mean he actually lived in sin with someone? *Here?* In Morristown?"

"Well, you couldn't really say that they lived together, either, considering she was gallivanting around the countryside three-fourths of the year."

"What do you mean? And who is *she*, anyway?"

"Jodi Forest," Kelly answered. "He met her at Arkansas State when he was going to college and—"

"And," interrupted Susan, "the summer after they graduated, they took off together to see the world. Walked all the way to California. But that fall he came back without her. The next spring she showed up again. Spent the whole summer on his farm. You know, the McElroy place. It belonged to his grandparents."

"Oh, yes. I remember them," Lara began. "They—"

"Well, they really aren't that important. They were dead by then."

"Anyway," Kelly said, taking over the storytelling, "she stayed the whole summer and then took off again the next fall. She came and went that way every year till this one. This year the whole summer went by without a sign of her. Jodi finally showed up in October, but she didn't even spend one night. She left town again the very same day she got here!"

"Couldn't have picked a worse time," Susan mused. "I mean this summer was hard enough on all the farmers, what with the drought and all. To up and leave the guy during a time like that... Well, he's better off without her."

"He certainly is, and so are we. Now one of us has a chance to grab him." Kelly grinned.

"Now wait a second." Lara held up one hand. "Why did she only stay for the summer, and what happened this year to change things?"

Susan looked at Kelly, who could only shrug her shoulders. "I guess Tanner is the only one that knows that."

"I'm astounded," Lara said. "You mean someone in Morristown was actually able to keep a secret for, what? Seven, eight years, at least?"

"Well, no one really knows much about Jodi, since she wasn't from here. She didn't spend much time in town, and she certainly didn't make an effort to be social," Susan said, excusing the lapse in the town's usually reliable communications network.

"And Tanner always has been more of the strong, silent type," Kelly added.

At that all three turned once more to study their conversation piece, only to find that he seemed to be equally fascinated with them.

Tanner was staring with obvious interest. His head was cocked at an angle, as if to catch whatever Beau the bartender was saying without having to take his eyes off them.

"He must be asking about Lara," Susan whispered. "He already knows who we are."

"Damn," Kelly swore, "I might have known a pretty young thing would move back into town, just when I finally have a chance at that guy. It's not fair, Lara. You and Susan have already tried marriage once. I ought to get to sample it before you two go back for seconds."

"Oh, Kelly, hush. For all you know he might just be asking if you brought a date to the Christmas party. Besides, if you don't know what happened, how do you know they broke up?"

"Tanner has never been known as a drinker, and he never even looked at another woman after he became involved with Jodi. Not even during all those months she was gone. He would just stay at home, waiting for her to come back.

"But ever since that day in October he has been getting drunk as a skunk practically every night, and the boys say he's been going to Memphis and tackling anything in a skirt."

"I guess he is not very impressed with the local talent." Susan sighed.

"Make that wasn't, as in past tense. Lara seems to have changed his mind." Kelly nodded toward the man in question. "Here he comes now. Looks like this is your lucky night, Lara."

Lara glanced up to see that Tanner was indeed headed toward them, a drink in each hand and his eyes fixed on her.

The scrape of chairs on the floor instantly brought her attention back to her friends. "Wait, you can't desert me now!"

"Now, Lara, it's okay. You may be playing out of turn, but we'll still be good sports about it," Kelly said as she and Susan hurriedly vacated their seats, generously leaving the field open for their friend.

"Terrific," Lara groaned. Good-looking though Tanner was, the last thing she needed was a drunk on the rebound. But before she could retreat herself, the tall farmer was standing in front of her, thoroughly blocking all routes for escape.

"Hello."

Lara swallowed hard. Damn, he had a sexy voice, even if it was a little slurred.

"Mind if I sit down?"

She meant to say the seats were taken, but somehow found herself gesturing toward the chair next to hers. "No, of course not."

Tanner started to grab the chair and pull it out, but he had both hands full. He glanced back and forth between the glasses and the chair, obviously perplexed.

"Let me get the chair for you," Lara finally offered.

"No, no. I can manage."

"Well, then perhaps I could take the drinks off your hands."

"No, thanks. I can handle them."

Tanner studied the situation for a few more moments before his face brightened, as if, indeed, a light bulb had been switched on inside his handsome head.

Carefully maintaining his balance on one foot, he stuck out the other, hooking the toe of his boot behind one chair leg. Slowly he pulled the chair back and then, in a sudden flurry of movement, slid his six-foot-two-inch frame into the seat, somehow managing to accomplish the feat without spilling too much of the drinks. When at last he managed to sit up straight and successfully place both glasses on the table, he flashed Lara a huge smile of triumph.

"You did that very well," Lara congratulated him, unable to hold back a smile of her own. Tanner's pride in having succeeded at such a simple thing reminded her so much of her two-year-old nephew.

"Thank you," he answered, quite seriously. "I've been practicing."

Lara laughed out loud this time. "It shows."

Tanner pushed one glass across the table toward her. "I brought this one for you."

"Thank you." She automatically accepted the drink, grimacing when she realized that it was straight whiskey. "But maybe you should keep it. I really think I've reached my limit."

"You sure? You seem okay to me."

"Yes, well, perhaps I don't handle alcohol quite as well as you do." She let him take the glass back, feeling a little guilty as Tanner quickly downed his own drink, then took hers and did the same. Somehow it seemed like giving water to a person in danger of drowning.

Setting the empty glasses on the table, he turned to stare silently at Lara. She smiled encouragingly, waiting for him to introduce himself, but Tanner seemed to have swallowed his powers of speech along with the whiskey. He just sat and stared.

"I'm Lara Jamison," she finally offered. He nodded.

"And you are—" She paused, offering him an opening.

But he just kept staring with a wistful, bemused expression.

"Tanner McNeil, right?"

He smiled, nodding slightly, as if he wasn't really paying attention to what she was saying.

Giving up on conversation, Lara wondered helplessly what to do with him. Usually she wouldn't even waste time trying to converse with someone who didn't know when to say when, but Tanner was such a sweet drunk. And, she remembered, he was going through a tough breakup. His relationship with Jodi had lasted longer than her marriage, and she was sure its ending must have been just as traumatic for him as divorce had been for her.

She was shaken out of her thoughts by the feel of rough, callused fingers gently grasping strands of her hair. Lara turned her head slightly to feel the warmth of his palm. Looking into his eyes, she realized that Tanner had become lost in a bittersweet memory. She lifted her hands to hold his against her cheek as she slowly opened his fingers.

"Tanner," she called softly, bringing him back to the present. "I think maybe you've had enough tonight. Let me get someone to drive you home, okay?"

Sparks of fire returned to the shimmering, gold eyes. "No," he said. "You won't come."

"Yes, I will," Lara promised, deciding on the spot. "In fact, I'll take you there myself. I think I can remember the way."

Holding on to both of his hands, she stood and began tugging him to his feet. "Come on, Tanner. I'm taking you home."

"Will you stay?" he asked.

"Not tonight, Tanner. Now come on. Let me drop you off."

She'd almost had him on his feet, when he sank back again so suddenly that she landed in his lap.

"Tanner!"

He looked at her with the saddest eyes she had ever seen and shook his head. "You won't stay."

"Well, maybe for just a little while. Come on," she pleaded, struggling to an upright position.

"Not good enough. I want you to stay."

Lara shook her head. "Not this time, Tanner. You're in no condition, anyway. Now come on and let me take you home, okay?"

As she pulled him to his feet again, Tanner placed one arm around her shoulders, letting her support his weight. Bearing her burden well, Lara headed for the exit, where they were met by Susan and Kelly.

"Lara, are you sure you know what you're doing?"

"Oh, Susan, I'm just taking him home, where he can sleep it off without us worrying about him being out there behind the wheel."

"She won't stay," Tanner told her friends sadly. "I asked her, but she still won't stay."

"He's wasted. Just ignore him," Lara said. "Tomorrow he probably won't even remember who I am."

"Are you sure you can handle him by yourself? Maybe I should come with you?" Kelly offered.

Lara knew she should say yes, but somehow felt that Tanner was her responsibility. She wanted to take care of him herself.

"Thanks, Kelly, but I can manage."

"Maybe she should go, Lara. In fact, maybe we should both go with you. Alcohol can do strange things to people."

"Now don't be silly, Susan. Tanner obviously isn't capable of hurting a fly. I'm just going to drop him off and then go on home myself. Stop worrying, okay?"

Reluctantly the women stepped aside, holding the door open so Lara could steer Tanner outside and over to her car. "I'll call you both tomorrow," she promised. "Now go on in and enjoy the Christmas party."

But Kelly and Susan continued to stand in the doorway, watching as Lara helped Tanner into the passenger seat of her car. "Just my luck," Kelly murmured. "Of all the old friends who could have moved back, it has to be a divorced blonde. Did you notice the way he touched her hair?"

"Uh-huh. You know, with it all crimped like that, Lara's hair looks a lot like Jodi's," Susan said.

"She won't stay. I asked her, but she still won't stay." Kelly repeated Tanner's words. "That's what he said. Susan, you don't think he thinks she's Jodi?"

"In his condition, who knows? It's certainly possible."

"Lara! Lara! Wait!" Kelly launched herself toward the car, but Lara had already started it up and begun to pull away, clearly not even seeing Kelly in the rearview mirror. All her friend's thoughts were probably centered on the sad, silent man beside her, Kelly decided.

"Kelly, come on. I'm sure she'll be fine," Susan called to the woman standing in the middle of the parking lot. Reluctantly Kelly returned to the club door.

"I just thought we should warn her. I mean, if he does think she's Jodi, Tanner might get really angry or something."

Susan patted her friend's shoulder in a comforting gesture. "Well, you tried your best. Don't worry. Lara's been living in the big, bad city. I'm sure she's learned to take care of herself. Besides, you said yourself that Tanner is the quiet type. She'll be fine."

"I said the strong, silent type, but I'm sure you're right." Nevertheless they both felt worried as they watched the lights of Lara's car disappear into the night.

As SHE HEADED down Highway One, Lara tried to recall the once familiar landmarks of her hometown. "Susan said you had taken over your grandparent's farm, the old McElroy place. That's off of Route Seven, isn't it, Tanner?"

"Hmm? Yes, that's right."

Lara sighed in relief. At least he hadn't passed out on her. Maybe she should keep him talking, to make sure he stayed awake until she got him home.

"You might need to help me out with directions. It's been a long time since I lived here."

"I know," Tanner said. "You didn't come this summer."

"That's right," Lara said, surprised that he even knew she was supposed to. "I had to stay on in Houston to finish up a big case I was handling. I had hoped to at least make it by fall. That's always been my favorite season here. Having a real fall was one of the things I missed most about home. Arkansas must be the most beautiful place in the world in autumn."

"Sad."

"Excuse me?"

"Autumn is sad. Everything changes. Leaves."

"Yes, the leaves do change. That's what makes it so beautiful. I don't think that's sad."

"No, everything leaves. Goes away. Sad."

Of course, Lara thought. Jodi had left him in October. She had always left in the fall, according to the girls. It really must have been a sad time for Tanner.

Lara reached over and placed her hand on top of his. "There is a time for every season, Tanner. And each season brings changes. Things will change for the better soon, I promise."

Tanner shook his head. "Nothing changes. I'm still alone."

"No, you aren't." Lara squeezed his hand firmly. "I'm here, and I'll always be here when you need someone to talk to, Tanner. I promise."

"You'll stay here?"

"Yes, Tanner. I'm here to stay for good. It took me a while to realize it, but Morristown is my home. You know, I used to tell people that Arkansas was a wonderful place to grow up or grow old, but there wasn't anything to do in the between time. But there isn't any between time, is there? We're always doing one or the other."

"You should stay."

Lara smiled across at him, giving his hand another pat as she slowed to make the turn that would take them to the McElroy farm. "I am staying, Tanner. Count on it."

Tanner turned his hand over so that their palms touched, threading his fingers through hers. "I'll make sure you stay this time."

She liked the feel of his hand around hers. She liked the sound of possessiveness she heard in his voice. In fact, Lara thought, she could get to like everything about this man, if he proved to be as endearing sober as he was drunk. Coming home had definitely been the right decision.

On that thought she pulled to a stop in front of the farmhouse. "Okay, Tanner, we're here." With obvious reluctance he released Lara's hand so she could shift into Park. "Do you think you can get out by yourself?"

"Hmm. Oh, yeah, I think so," he said, sitting perfectly still.

"Here, why don't we start by undoing your seat belt?" Lara pressed the button releasing the shoulder harness and guided the strap back across Tanner's chest.

As she leaned toward him, he reached out once more to touch her hair, then let his finger slide gently down her neck and across her throat. Lara held her breath as he hesitated, a puzzled look on his face.

"It's gone."

"What, Tanner? What's gone?"

But he shook his head. "Doesn't matter. You won't be going away anymore. You're here to stay." Then he smiled and really took her breath away. She definitely could get to like this man.

"That's right, I'm here to stay. Come on, I'll walk you to your door." Lara got out on her side, then went around to help him out. He wrapped his arm around her shoulders again, although he didn't lean on her as heavily. Together they made it up the steps and came to a stop at the door.

"Do you have your keys?"

"Not locked."

"What? Oh, sorry, I forgot where we were. I guess some readjustments take a little longer." Twisting the knob, she pushed the door open and ushered Tanner inside.

"I guess you can make it on your own from here. Be sure and drink lots of water and take some aspirin before you go to sleep. It'll help the hangover you're going to have in the morning."

Turning to face him, she hesitated only briefly, then stood on her toes to brush a soft kiss across his lips. "It was nice meeting you, Tanner. Don't forget to call me. I'm a good listener."

Lara pulled back, intending to leave, but Tanner plainly had other ideas. His arm tightened around her. "You said you were staying."

"I am going to stay. I told you Morristown is my home."

"No." Tanner raised his other arm so that she was standing in the circle of his embrace. "You're staying with me."

Lara felt the steel in his arms as she read the expression of determination on his face and knew that she could be in big trouble.

"No, Tanner. I said I was staying in this town. Not with you. We already discussed this back at the club."

"You're not leaving me again. I won't let you."

"Again? I don't understand." But even as she said the words, Lara did understand. Gently she raised her hands, placing them on either side of his face. "Look at me, Tanner. I'm Lara, not Jodi."

"Lara?" The fog seemed to lift, and Tanner found himself looking into eyes that were as green as grass in springtime, not the pale blue of a summer sky. He felt the body he was pressing against his and realized that it was soft and full. Not lean and hardened by thousands of miles of travel.

"No, you're not Jodi. She left. You're staying."

"That's right, Tanner. I'm staying, and we will have plenty of time to get to know each other. Everything will be fine, you'll see."

Lara stepped back as Tanner let his arms fall to his sides, reminding her again of a small child. Treating him as such, she led him to what appeared to be his room. Pushing him down onto the bed, she removed his shoes and loosened his clothing. Then she pulled a quilt up to cover him. His eyes were already closed when she bent over to kiss him gently once more.

"Lara," he repeated sleepily.

"That's right, Tanner. I am Lara."

2

TANNER WOKE UP SLOWLY, aware that he had a hangover even before he opened his eyes. He had had enough of them recently to recognize the pounding in his head and the dryness of his mouth. He also recognized the feel of the bed and the sounds coming from outside his window, and knew that at least he was in his own room. What he wasn't sure of was whether or not he was alone.

He had some vague recollection of seeing Jodi, but that wasn't unusual. For some reason, all women looked like Jodi when he'd had enough to drink.

He had lost count of the number of times he'd gotten wasted since October. At first he had just gone out with the intention of sleeping with as many women as it took to forget her. It hadn't taken long for him to realize that he couldn't even get interested in another woman until he was too drunk to remember if anything had actually happened. By that time his vision was too blurred to really see what the woman looked like, so his mind automatically filled in the blanks with Jodi's image, defeating his purpose entirely.

Something had been different last night, though. He wasn't sure what and was afraid that if he opened his eyes, he might find out. He had woken up in plenty of strange bedrooms in the past two months, but nothing had frightened him as much as waking up here, in the house he had shared every summer with Jodi. Tanner had never brought anyone else to his home, afraid he would be completely unable to perform in a house filled with reminders.

Trying to think in spite of the headache, he realized that there was no sense of a body lying next to him. No flesh touching his. No dent in the mattress. No warmth from a sleeping body. Maybe whoever had been with him had already left.

Cautiously opening one eye, he searched what little of the room he could see for clues. There were none. No pieces of feminine clothing lying on the floor. In fact, there were no masculine pieces, either. Turning his head slightly, he studied the pattern of his shirt sleeve and realized that he was still fully dressed. Obviously nothing had happened, but he still felt fairly sure that he hadn't come home alone.

Opening both eyes now, he scanned the entire room, letting his gaze finally come to rest on the nightstand beside him. Whomever he'd brought home was a person worth keeping, he decided, reaching out to grab the aspirin bottle and glass of water that had been placed on the table. Lifting them up, he also discovered the note that had been lying beneath. Setting the water back down, he took the note and studied it carefully.

Take three aspirin, drink plenty of water and call me in the morning.

Lara.
296-4245

He swallowed the aspirins with all of the water, then reread the note. Lara. She had been at the Jubilee, talking to Susan Metcalf and Kelly Ryan. He thought she had hair like Jodi's, but that might just be the whiskey. Then he remembered the eyes. Grass green, not sky blue. Maybe he was getting over Jodi, after all.

Sitting up slowly, he swung his feet to the floor. He stretched as he stood, wincing at the creak of joints and bones. At thirty-two he was hardly over the hill, he just felt wasted. Not drunk; wasted. Wasted, as in misspent, badly used, thrown away.

A brief tour of the house assured him that whoever Lara was, she had indeed left. Running a hand through his hair, he stumbled toward the bathroom and the promise of a hot shower. Maybe he would be able to remember more, once he started to look and feel like a human again.

In the middle of his shower it dawned on him that Lara couldn't have left without a car. He walked out to the front porch, nothing but a towel wrapped around his waist. There was no sign of another car, and his pickup truck was missing.

Either this Lara had stolen his truck, or it was sitting in the parking lot of the Jube. Somehow he doubted that Susan the newspaper editor or Kelly the band director would be associating with a car thief.

Going back inside, he walked over to the phone and dialed the private club. No answer. Belatedly he realized that it was Sunday and the club wouldn't be open again until Tuesday night. He drummed his fingers impatiently on the telephone. There had been a number after Lara's name.

Once more in the bedroom, he picked up the note for the second time. Just holding it gave him goose bumps. Of course, he mocked himself, they *might* also be due to the fact that he hadn't dried off yet; it was awfully cold. Putting the note aside, he toweled his body dry and slipped into a clean pair of jeans and a plaid flannel shirt.

Taking the slip of paper with him, he went to the kitchen and started the coffee maker. Laying the note on the table, he busied himself making breakfast, knowing that he was stalling, but unable to act. The unknown Lara frightened him. He desperately needed someone who could make him forget Jodi; at the same time, he was afraid of getting involved with a woman who held that kind of power. Damn. He wished he could remember more.

He polished off his breakfast absentmindedly, hardly aware of what he was eating. Automatically he got up and washed his dishes, then poured himself another cup of coffee.

Kelly or Susan would probably be delighted to fill him in about Lara, but he really didn't want to involve them. Both women had been very kind to him, after the town realized that Jodi hadn't stayed this time. Each had subtly indicated that they would be willing to help ease the ache. Tempting as their offers were, Tanner hadn't wanted to go to someone he might come to like.

Chasing women he could never care for had seemed the best way to vent his frustration and anger. But this morning he knew that had changed. The binges were over. Now it was time to look for a different sort of answer.

Knowing the decision had been made, he set down the coffee cup and picked up Lara's note. He took it over to the phone and dialed the number she had printed after her name.

The phone rang once, twice, three times. He decided he would give it two more rings before he hung up. Four. Five, and she answered.

"Hello."

He almost hung up, anyway. Almost.

"Hello, is anyone there?"

"Lara?" he said hesitantly. The husky, feminine voice didn't bring back any memories, but it definitely stirred up the longing to create some.

"Yes, this is Lara Jamison. May I ask who's calling?"

"Tanner McNeil." Damn, he thought, I should have rehearsed.

But Lara easily filled in the blanks for him.

"I hope you're feeling all right this morning. You went out like a light almost as soon as you got home. Did you take the aspirin?"

"Yes, thank you. It was very thoughtful of you to put them beside the bed."

"Well, I've had a few hangovers myself. Not many, but a few."

"Yeah, well, I guess I've been having a few too many lately."

"So I've heard."

Tanner winced at that. Of course, the whole town knew. Somehow he just hadn't cared what people might think until now. "I, uh, haven't exactly been myself."

Lara quickly put him at ease. "Hey, it's okay. We've all suffered from a broken heart at least once. Everyone understands, Tanner."

Obviously she knew about Jodi. Undoubtedly she hadn't hesitated to let Kelly and Susan fill her in. Tanner wished he had called one of the other women first. He was at a decided disadvantage. He would have given anything at that moment to know a little more about Lara.

"Tanner? Are you still there?"

"Yes, yes. I'm still here," he answered at last.

"Look, I just wanted you to know that if you'd like to talk or if you need anything, I'm here."

"Well, actually there is one thing. My truck."

"Your truck?"

"I, uh, guess it's still at the Jube."

"Oh, good heavens. I forgot all about that. You weren't exactly in shape to drive home, so I took you in my car. Look, I'll be there in twenty minutes and we'll go back and get your truck."

"Thanks. I really appreciate it. Last night, too."

"No problem. That's what friends are for, right? See you in a few minutes."

Tanner hung up the phone, a little dazed. Lara had treated him like an old friend, yet he couldn't remember any old friends named Lara. What had she given as her last name? James? No, Jamison. She couldn't be one of those Jamisons, could she? They'd all moved away.

There had been four kids in the family. He had been in the same class as the second daughter, Claire, and had played football with L.J., the only son. And there had been two other daughters. One older than Claire. Ellen or Elaine or something with an *E*. And there had been one younger. Lara? Everyone in town knew the family, or knew of them. They had all been over-achievers. Kids with potential. Every one of them had been selected as most likely to succeed and they had, but not surprisingly their success hadn't been found in Morristown.

The parents had moved to the resort community in the Ozarks developed by the father. L.J. had gone to Fayetteville on a football scholarship and was on the coaching staff there now. Everyone remembered him, especially when they wanted tickets to a Razorback game. The girls had all made it big in one way or another. Ellen or Elaine or something with an *E* had married well, someone in Jonesboro, and they owned their own business. Claire was some sort of vice president for a big company in Little Rock. The youngest—Lara?— had gone on to law school somewhere in Texas.

He vaguely remembered her saying something about Houston last night. Oh, yeah. She'd had to stay there longer than she'd planned, to finish up a big case. That was why she hadn't made it back in time for her favorite season, autumn. Well, he was glad it was somebody's favorite season. It sure wasn't his.

So Lara was the youngest Jamison. What on earth was she doing back in Morristown?

Before he could figure out the answer to that question, Tanner heard the sound of a car pulling up and went to the front door to greet the subject of his thoughts. He placed his hand on the knob, then hesitated, seeing once more the image he had created last night. He wondered how much of it was accurate and how much had been filled in by pieces of Jodi.

Taking a deep breath, he opened the door and found his answer. Lara had already gotten out of her car and was coming up the steps. The hair was blond all right, although merely wavy, and it was a shade darker, with just a hint of red. Strawberry, not corn silk. The body was undeniably attractive, although nothing like Jodi's taut, lean form.

For a split second Tanner remembered the soft fullness of the woman he had held in his arms last night.
No, the body was definitely not Jodi's, but it sure as hell
had felt good next to his. When she was standing directly in front of him, he saw her eyes. Grass green. Exactly as he'd remembered. That seemed terribly
significant, although he didn't know why.

"Hello."

Lara was pleased to discover his voice was just as
sexy when it wasn't slurred.

"Hi. How do you feel?"

"Probably not as bad as I deserve. Thanks for taking care of me last night. I'm afraid I didn't make a very
good first impression."

"Actually you were one of the nicest drunks I've ever
met. Believe me, if you hadn't been, I would have found
someone else to drive you home."

"Thank goodness I was on good behavior then. I
really appreciate you taking me to get the truck, too."

"It really isn't a problem. I should have asked Kelly
or Susan to drive yours home and then taken them back
to the club. They both offered to help."

"I'm just as glad you didn't. I wouldn't have had an
excuse to call you otherwise." Tanner blushed as he realized what he'd said. He didn't know where the words
were coming from. They just seemed to have a will of
their own.

"Then I'm glad, too. Come on, let's go."

Tanner pulled the door closed behind him and followed her to the bright red car, noticing for the first time
that it was a Mercedes. Feeling out of his league, he
said, "I guess the law business must be doing pretty
well."

Lara laughed easily. "Don't be too impressed. I bought it used, but don't tell anyone else. I wouldn't want to spoil my image."

The fact that it was used made Tanner feel a little better, but not much. A used Mercedes would still cost twice as much as a brand-new, four-wheel-drive pickup, and four times as much as his truck, which had also been purchased used.

Maybe six times, he amended, noting the leather seats as he got in. "Do you think lawyering in Arkansas is going to be as profitable as it was in Texas?" He winced as he heard the question come out. He sounded like some kind of gigolo, for crying out loud.

"Probably not," Lara said, "but that's okay. I've learned that a lot of other things are more important. A practice here should support me sufficiently, and I know it will be a lot more rewarding."

"Oh? In what way?"

Lara shrugged. "It's hard to put into words. I guess I just want to feel that I'm helping people, not just handling files. The firm I worked for in Houston handled a large volume of cases, and most of our clients were businesses, not individuals. It seemed…I don't know… abstract, impersonal, unimportant. The people here in Morristown are real to me. I've known most of them all my life. They aren't just another job number to bill hours to. They're people I care about."

"Is that why you decided to move back?"

"There were other reasons also."

"Such as?"

Lara laughed at his open curiosity. "What is this? An interrogation? Why don't we talk about you for a while?"

"Nothing to tell. Still in the same town. Still farming the land that's been in my mother's family for four generations. End of story."

"What about Jodi?"

Tanner ground his teeth, his hands clenched into fists. "Like I said, nothing to tell. How did you know about her, anyway?"

"Susan and Kelly told me. I understand that you were together a long time."

"Not exactly. She never stayed long. She only spent the summers here."

"But . . ."

"Look, Lara. I really don't want to talk about Jodi anymore. She won't be back this time, so why don't we both just forget her?"

"Well, that would be easy for me, Tanner. I've never even met her. I don't think it will be easy for you, though. It shouldn't be."

"You don't know anything about it."

Lara knew she was stirring up a hornet's nest, yet she still kept prodding. "No, I don't. But I do know what it's like to break up with someone you care about, to finally give up on a relationship you know isn't going to work."

"Do you?"

"Yes. My divorce became final two years ago. It took a long time to get over it and to get on with my life."

Tanner was surprised. "I didn't even know you'd been married."

"It seems that Morristown's communications network isn't what it used to be."

"What happened?"

She shook her head. "You don't really want to be bored with the details. Besides, we're here. There's your truck. Right where you left it."

To Tanner's surprise they were already in the Jubilee's parking lot. "I want to talk to you some more. Let's go get some coffee or something and then come back."

"Tanner."

"Please, Lara, I want to know what happened."

"Why?"

"I don't know. You said that you understand what I'm going through because you've been there. Maybe by hearing your story I'll understand it, too. I don't right now. Nothing seems to make sense anymore. Does it bother you to talk about it?"

"Oh, no. I'm long past that point."

Lara knew Tanner needed someone right now to help him see through the hurt. She also knew that she wanted to be the one to help him. She had already passed through all the phases of recovery, including the period when she had refused to talk to anyone and the times when she had needed to talk incessantly.

"All right. We'll go to Riley's for some coffee. Okay?"

"Fine," Tanner agreed, relieved to have her with him a little longer.

Riley's, being the only coffee shop in town, was packed, as always. The after-church crowd, dressed in their Sunday best, had taken over the formal dining room, leaving Lara and Tanner with a corner booth upfront by the café windows.

They settled in and ordered coffee, each silently staring out at the parking lot until the waitress had left.

"Tell me about it?" Tanner finally asked.

"What would you like to know?"

"Everything. Just start at the beginning."

"Okay. I was clerking for a law firm in Houston during the summer after my first year in law school. Kevin was—is—a private investigator. He was doing some consulting work on one of our cases. I was responsible for tracking down all the files and records he needed to further the investigation. We spent a lot of time together on the case and hit it off. I had never really been seriously involved with anyone before him. I guess it all sort of went to my head. The next thing I knew, we were living together. That fall I transferred to a law school in Houston. We got married during the next spring break."

"How long were you married?"

"Four years."

"No kids?"

She shook her head, frowning. "That was one of the things we disagreed on. I wanted a family, he didn't."

"You didn't discuss it before the wedding."

"Yes and no. It's hard to explain. I think Kevin and I had both reached a point where we really wanted to find the right person. Most of my friends back here were already married and having children. I hadn't even come close to the altar. Kevin was thirty-three, and while he had been involved plenty of times, it just never worked out. We were so relieved to find each other, someone that seemed to fit, I think we purposefully overlooked our differences." Lara paused a moment, carefully sipping her coffee.

"You have to understand that in a lot of ways we did seem exactly right for each other. Kevin wanted an independent woman. Someone who had a life and interests of her own. Here I was, a bright, young lawyer-to-be with a promising career. He used to be really proud of the fact that I was an attorney. It didn't even bother him that I wanted to keep my maiden name and establish my own line of credit. It struck him as being very modern, and that suited him. We had the marriage of the eighties, dual income, no kids.

"Then I realized that I wanted what he called a marriage of the fifties. A comfortable house, two kids, a dog, a cat and a joint banking account. Well, Kevin is afraid of dogs, and while he's great with our nieces and nephews, he didn't want to be tied down by the responsibility of having our own children. He finally agreed we could have a family eventually, when we could afford a full-time nanny to take care of them. But I couldn't see the point in having children, if you're just going to hire someone else to raise them for you."

Tanner signaled the waitress for more coffee. He studied Lara carefully while it was being poured, waiting until they were alone again to ask what he felt was an obvious question.

"I understand what attracted Kevin to you. But what attracted you to him?"

Lara was surprised. She had never had anyone ask that before. But then, most of her friends at the time of the divorce had known Kevin and wouldn't have had to ask. "Kevin loves life.

"I don't think I ever met anyone who had more enthusiasm for living. And it's contagious. When you're around him, he makes you want to see and do everything there is. He's one of the few men I've met who could actually enjoy a play or a ballet as much as a football game. He's always ready to go somewhere new or try something different. He's spontaneous."

Watching her smile as she described him, seeing the glow on her face, Tanner wondered if she wasn't still in love with him.

"Why did he leave?"

"He didn't, although people always assume that. I'm the one who left."

"Why? The way you described him just now, you made him sound wonderful."

"He is wonderful in a lot of ways. And I'll always love those qualities about him. It's just—" Lara sighed heavily "—it's just hard to explain."

Choosing her words carefully, she tried to make Tanner understand. "Kevin's other relationships didn't work out, because he couldn't find someone who loved life as much as he did, who wanted to live as fully as he tries to. Well, I do love life and I do want to live my life fully. It's just that I define that differently than he does."

Lara stopped, gathering her thoughts before going on. "My definition of a full life includes a home and a family. Kevin saw them as hindrances. He was attracted to me because I was independent. I wouldn't be a responsibility. But I wanted to be able to depend on someone, and I wanted that person to be able to depend on me in return. I wanted all the things that frightened him."

Tanner listened to what she was saying, painfully familiar with much of it. "So you stopped loving him."

"No, I didn't say that. I think in some ways I will always love Kevin. But you can't always live with someone you love. I love my parents, but I could never move back home with them. I love my sisters and brother, but we would drive each other nuts in the same house. I don't know how we managed while we were growing up.

"I love Kevin, but I can't live with him. We don't want the same things out of life. As long as we stayed together, we were both being shortchanged, because neither of us were able to have what we wanted. That's why I left."

"He didn't try to keep you?"

"He did at first, and then he realized I was right. As miserable as we both were after we first separated, we were still happier than we had been together."

"You never had second thoughts?"

"Oh sure! Second, third and fourth thoughts." Lara turned her head to stare out the window, ashamed of what she was about to tell him. "I even begged him to take me back at one point. I was afraid of being alone again. But by then Kevin had also realized we didn't belong together. He tried to be nice about it, but the answer was a flat no."

"What did you do?"

"I cried buckets, swore I hated him and then thanked the Lord that he hadn't said yes. We just would have had to go through the whole separation all over again later on."

"You really believe that?"

Lara looked straight into his eyes this time. "Yes, I really believe that. Oh, I still get down sometimes, Tanner. And I get scared. I think, what if I never find the person who's right for me? Wouldn't being with someone who was almost right be enough?"

"And?"

"It wouldn't be. 'Almost' only counts in horseshoes. I hope I will find the right person. But if I don't, I'm still happy with the life I'm carving for myself. It may not include everything I want, but it's mine and of my own making. When I'm miserable, that's my own making, too, and not because I'm depending on someone else to be something they can't be."

"Which brings us to the moral of our story," Tanner said.

"And the conclusion of story hour," Lara agreed. "Let's go pick up your truck."

As they drove past the law office on the corner, Tanner noticed that the sign had been changed from William J. Harris, Attorney at Law to Harris and Jamison, Attorneys at Law.

"You're going into practice with Bill Harris?"

"That's right. He used to handle all the paperwork for Dad's real-estate transactions. I talked to him a lot about the possibility of going to law school when I was growing up. The last time I was home for a visit, he asked me if I'd like to join him and handle the family law and litigation cases. He prefers to stick to real-estate and business deals."

"So you really are planning to stay here for good?" Tanner asked.

"That's right. There's no place like home. Trust me, I've looked."

Tanner smiled. "So have I, and I couldn't agree more."

Lara turned into the Jubilee's parking lot again and pulled up beside his truck. "Well, here we are."

"Thanks for the ride, Lara. And the story. I know it really wasn't any of my business."

"Don't be silly. Next time it'll be your turn to do the telling. Then we'll be even."

Tanner grimaced. "You may have to wait awhile. I haven't figured out the ending to mine yet. Much less the moral."

"That's okay. You will soon enough. Call me if I can help. You've got my number?"

"I've got it."

"Good. Don't lose it."

"I won't," he promised. Then swiftly, before he could change his mind, he leaned forward and kissed her. When he drew back at last, he had to laugh at her astonished expression. "Watch out, Miss Lara. Kevin's not the only one who can be spontaneous."

He was out of the car before she recovered her senses. Her mind was still blank when he honked and waved before pulling out onto the street.

Then she smiled, remembering all those friends in Houston who thought she was going to be bored in Morristown.

3

IT HAD BEEN a long time since Tanner had asked a woman out. He tried calling Lara at least a dozen times during the week before Christmas, but he always hung up before he had even finished dialing her number. Where does a guy over eighteen take a date in Morristown, Arkansas, population 7,356 and still growing?

He hadn't dated anyone but Jodi since his freshman year in college, and there had been fraternity dances and ball games to go to then. If it had still been football season, he supposed he could have asked her to the Friday night, high school game. Everyone in town went. But the season had ended six weeks ago, and basketball games wouldn't resume till mid-January, three weeks away.

The only movie theater in town had closed down five years ago. If they wanted to go to a movie, they would have to drive all the way to Jonesboro or Memphis, Tennessee, both an hour away. That meant he would have two hours in total, where they would have nothing but each other for entertainment while he drove. Lara seemed easy to talk to, but she might ask questions about Jodi, and he wasn't ready to talk yet.

So where does a man take a woman when he wants to spend time with her, but doesn't want to make conversation? He liked the obvious answer, but doubted that Lara would go for it. Of course, there were holiday parties being thrown by friends, but most of those were too small and intimate. He needed someplace crowded and noisy first.

Morristown was located in a dry county, which meant there were no liquor stores, and the only places allowed to serve alcohol were the two private clubs. Tanner couldn't afford the country club's membership fee, and the Jubilee, which everyone of legal age in three counties belonged to, was booked solid for private parties up till Christmas Eve. Then it closed for a week, not reopening till New Year's Eve, when it held a big party for all the members.

The only options left were the church socials. There was an official decree that all church events in Morristown were multidenominational. In a community where social activities were limited, the citizens made the most of each occasion regardless of who was sponsoring it. So the Methodists went to the Baptist revivals, and Baptists and Methodists went to the dances held at the Knights of Columbus Hall. There was also a bus that went to the synagogue in Memphis every Saturday, and anyone willing to contribute a dollar to the gas tank was welcome to ride along.

The church socials were crowded and noisy and the entertainment was free, but, well, they didn't exactly set the stage for seduction.

He would just have to settle for New Year's Eve at the Jube, Tanner decided. It seemed a long time away, but it was still two weeks sooner than the next basketball game, and it did meet all the requirements. Now he had to figure out when to ask Lara.

If he called too soon, she might suggest doing something between now and then, and he would be back in the same fix. If he waited too long, though, someone else might ask her first, and then he would be spending New Year's Eve by himself. He was determined not to spend the night alone with nothing to do but think of Jodi, as he had for the past seven years. This would be the start of not just a new year, but a new life, and Tanner wanted to begin as he aimed to continue.

Meanwhile, Lara was sitting in her law office, wondering why the heck Tanner hadn't called. She had thought about calling him several times, but every time she picked up the phone, she heard a mental recording of all her mother's lectures about why girls didn't call boys. Finally, on Christmas Eve morning, Lara decided she had never listened to her mother before, so why should she start now?

TANNER PUT DOWN the stack of underwear he'd been about to pack and reached for the phone, expecting Samantha to be on the other end. She always wanted to know the minute he was leaving. Samantha was very practical.

"Ten forty-five."

"Excuse me?"

"This isn't Samantha?"

"No, it's Lara."

"Lara? Lara! I'm sorry. I was expecting someone else."

"You mean Samantha?"

"Yeah, she usually calls to see what time I'm leaving. Wants to know when she has to start worrying about me."

"I see. Well, I won't keep you, then."

"Oh, hey, don't hang up. She'll try back if she gets a busy signal. Sam never gives up. You know how sisters are."

"Sam's your sister?"

"Big sister, second mother. Same thing."

"Say no more. I have two of them and a big brother. Sometimes I think I'm really an only child with five parents."

Tanner laughed. "I know the feeling."

"Are you going to her house for Christmas?"

"Yes. She and her family live in Little Rock."

"Will you be gone long?" Lara asked, wondering if her mother was going to be proven right yet again.

"No longer than absolutely necessary. Two or three days in that loony bin is all I can handle."

"Your Christmas sounds a lot like mine. Everyone's meeting at Mom and Dad's and it's guaranteed to drive a sane person mad. And don't tell me I have nothing to worry about. I've heard it before."

"I would never say such a thing. My mother and sister raised a gentleman."

"Meaning you might think it, but you're too polite to say so."

"Exactly."

"Well, it so happens I am looking for just such a gentleman to escort me to the New Year's Eve party at the Jubilee. I, uh, don't suppose you know where I might find one?"

"Madam, your search is over. I know just such a gentleman and he is I or I am him, whichever."

"Well, would you and he or him and you like to pick me up at eight o'clock?"

"We shall be delighted. In fact, we were just getting ready to call you with the same invitation."

"Oh, really?" she asked doubtfully.

"Really." Tanner dropped the humor and added in all seriousness, "I have wanted to see you, Lara. I don't know how many times I've picked up the phone. But well, it's been a long time since I dated anyone. I guess I am feeling a little rusty."

"That's all right, I understand. I'm glad I called. I'll be looking forward to New Year's Eve."

"Me, too. Merry Christmas, Lara."

"Merry Christmas. Drive safely."

"I will. Goodbye."

Tanner held on to the phone for a moment, waiting to hear the click of disconnection before he lowered the receiver into its cradle. He was glad she had called. Jodi had always been afraid to make the first move. She had a fear of being rejected that he'd never understood, yet she thought nothing of the chances she took, traveling alone through foreign lands, with hardly a cent to her name.

He was beginning to realize what a mystery Jodi had been. Trying to fathom her had been a challenge at first, then it had just become a frustration. She hadn't trusted him enough to open up. Sometimes he had wondered if she really loved him at all, or if he was just some sort of safe harbor, where she could rest and store up energy before she traveled on to distant shores.

Well, he decided, whatever he had been to her, he was no more. Now was the time to look into the future and, since Lara had arrived, the future sure looked a whole lot brighter. He laughed when he realized that he had learned more about her from two phone calls and a cup of coffee than he had from Jodi in seven years.

Lara wanted many of the same things that he did, such as a home with children and a loving spouse, in a town where both their families had put down roots. She was obviously willing to take her share of risks when it came to establishing a relationship, or she wouldn't have called him.

Of course, there was always the possibility that she simply felt sorry for him, but Tanner didn't think that was the case. No woman took the risk of calling a man who had ignored her for over a week, just because she felt sorry for him.

It dawned on him then how insensitive he had been. He'd been so wrapped up in trying to protect his own hide that he hadn't even thought about Lara's feelings. Hell, he had kissed her that day in the parking lot and then taken off, never to be heard from again. He'd been a real jerk, and still she had called him.

No, Lara definitely did not feel sorry for him. Tanner smiled for the first time in days. He would make it up to her on New Year's Eve. Shoot, at this rate he might even propose. If they could get this far over a couple of cups of coffee, there was no telling what they could accomplish in a whole night together.

That bit of imagining kept him smiling all the way to Little Rock and through the entire Christmas holiday. He didn't even get mad at Samantha when she got in her "I told you so"s about Jodi. Tanner had a new woman to dream about, a whole new life to plan. His New Year's resolution was to pretend Jodi had never even existed. He was sure he could keep it, if he just concentrated hard enough on Lara.

WHEN TANNER WOKE UP New Year's Eve morning, he realized that he had left one thing out of his imaginings—the weather. He woke to a winter wonderland, its white overcoat growing thicker by the minute. It finally quit snowing at noon, deciding to sleet instead.

The power and phone lines were down by three o'clock. At four the radio declared it the worst blizzard Arkansas had seen in this century, and the disc jockey announced that both the Jubilee and the country club had canceled their parties.

Tanner was pissed. Mother Nature had to pick the first New Year's Eve in seven years on which he had a date to be a party pooper. At five o'clock he quit kicking the furniture and started hitting the bottle instead. At six o'clock he realized that drinking was only making him feel worse, and he hadn't thought that was possible.

By the time his grandmother's clock struck seven, he was layered in practically every warm piece of clothing he owned. His four-wheel-drive, all-terrain vehicle was warmed up, and after putting on his crash helmet and gloves, Tanner was ready to go.

He had briefly considered taking the pickup, but had decided it would already be next year before he got the chains on the tires. Besides, he couldn't pick it up and pull it out of the ditch or ditches that he had no doubt he was about to slide into.

It was crazy even to think about going. He knew it had to be at least ten miles to the Jamison family home where Lara was staying, probably closer to fifteen. But even knowing that his chances were slim and only a fool would attempt it, he left. If this was the first night of the rest of his life, he would rather go down trying than spend one more miserable moment alone, pining for something that was not meant to be.

The ATV performed fairly well going down the gravel road that took him from the farm to Highway One. It was illegal to drive the vehicle on the highway, but Tanner figured that even if Sheriff Campbell and his men were crazy enough to be out on a night like this, they would probably be on his side. *All the world loves a lover,* he reminded himself.

He met the first ditch coming around the bend at Harold's Corner. Just a few bruises, nothing serious. He met the second one where Highway One met Business Route One, forming what the juveniles in town commonly referred to as the Loop. At that point he decided he had had enough of the highway and began to cut through town, using the side streets.

Two hours and too many spills to count later, he was sitting at the bottom of Sunset Hill. He was at the bottom, because after ten tries, the closest to the top he had come was still two-thirds down. He would have gone around the hill, except that Lara's house was sitting right on its highest point.

Abandoning the ATV altogether, he decided to attack the steep slope on foot. Fortunately Mrs. Jamison loved trees and had insisted that the woods be left intact, even if they did obscure a beautiful view of Morristown. Tanner began to pull himself up the hill, one tree at a time, until at last he stood outside the French doors that opened on to the rear deck.

Removing his crash helmet, he stood, staring through the paned windows. Lara lay on the floor in front of the fireplace. Looking beautiful, soft and warm, she quietly fed the fire, unwittingly also fanning the flames of desire that were already licking at every single nerve in his body.

Tanner forgot the bruises and scratches he had acquired. He forgot even the bitter cold and the dampness that were seeping through all the layers of clothing. The only thing he was capable of feeling now was the flare of passion igniting his soul. He had never wanted a woman so much, so desperately.

Lara slowly became aware of a new heat reaching out to her, hotter than any fire could possibly be. She turned at last and saw Tanner on the other side of the window. He pressed his hand against the glass separating them, as if he expected it to melt away like ice under the force of the sun.

She should have been startled, but was not. His presence was merely an extension of her thoughts. He had already been in her mind and heart. Now he was here physically and their union could be complete.

Lara opened the doors and brought him into her arms, knowing that however briefly they had known each other, whatever obstacles remained in their way, tonight this was where he belonged.

He stripped away his coveralls and gloves, then impatiently kicked off his boots. The sweater and wool shirt vanished, together with the jeans and long johns. Her robe slid to the floor. Tanner lifted her satin gown up and over her head, sending it flying across the room along with any inhibitions that might have remained.

She led him to the hearth, bringing him down to lie beside her on the plush rug. The mammoth, stone fireplace provided a glow that surrounded them, but Tanner knew Lara was the true source of the heat flowing through his veins. He was drawn to her as a moth to a flame and was past caring whether the fire consumed him.

They spoke not a word, saying all they felt with eyes that could not look away and lips that clung helplessly. Ever so slowly his hands searched each and every feminine curve and hollow, memorizing each secret by touch alone.

Unable to lie still beneath his fingers, Lara began her own exploration. Leaving a trail of hot, moist kisses, she traced the path from his firm jawline to the hollow of his neck, then lower still to the rigid nipples she knew must ache to be suckled as much as her own did.

His body tense and trembling, Tanner shuddered as he felt her teeth nibbling at him. The pleasure was almost more than he could endure. Then she moved lower. She licked and sucked and stroked every naked inch from his chest to his toes. Every inch, except those that begged for her attention the most.

Then she pushed her way between his thighs, kneeling over him, letting her breasts brush against the one area she had neglected with her mouth and hands. At last she lowered her head, nipping at the insides of his thighs, working around to the heavy sacs, then placing her tongue on the pulsing vein that carried his life force and following it up the rock-hard shaft to the pinnacle, where one tiny bead of moisture already shimmered.

He knew what she was going to do next but, badly though he wanted her to, he could bear it no longer. Tanner lifted her up to return the pleasure she had given him, ounce for ounce. He tasted the ripe fullness of her breasts, the sweetness of her flesh, and finally the tangy dew between her thighs. Lara cried out, unable to hold back the flood of passion that was raging through her body.

He tried to enter her slowly, knowing she was straining to receive him. But Lara didn't want him to hold back. She slid her hands from his shoulders, letting him feel the edge of her nails as her fingers skidded down his back, before sinking into the flesh at his hips. Using all the strength she possessed, she pulled him inside, surging upward to encase him completely in the snug channel carved as if just for this man's body.

Tanner surrendered. Unable to control the needs that drove him, he thrust even deeper, withdrawing and repeating the movement again and again. Each time faster and harder and deeper than the time before. Faster and harder and deeper, until he burst through the boundaries of pain and pleasure, soaring higher and freer than he had ever flown before, carrying Lara with him.

Drifting down gently, slowly, once more they landed softly on the warm rug in front of the dying fire and lay quietly, until the warmth of the hearth was just a memory. Then Lara rose, leading him through the dark and up the stairs to her bedroom.

He stood in the doorway, watching as she spread an extra quilt on top of the bed, then pulled back the covers so they could crawl in. She turned to him, still naked, still beautiful, and as he walked toward her he knew that the loving wasn't over yet. Already he felt a new hunger for her. A desire to make love again, slowly this time, ever so slowly.

They never heard the sirens at midnight. Nor did they see the fireworks someone set off down below. They had eyes and ears only for each other.

When Tanner fell asleep at last, Lara held him in her arms, his head lying on her breasts. He was hers. This was the man she had been destined to love. She had found him. Now she had only to find a way to keep him.

4

GRAPHIC IMAGES of a man and woman intimately entwined filled Lara's mental picture screen in vivid detail. Desperately she tried to focus on something, anything else. But last night's love scenes were the only show on, and Lara could not turn off the visions.

Damn Emma for making up that stupid game. Her big sister, hoarse from reading too many stories aloud, had taught a young Lara to create her own magical television that didn't have to be turned off at bedtime. The screen would appear when she closed her eyes. The channel could be changed with just a twist of her ear.

Lara had stopped pushing her nose to turn on this "TV" years ago. However, she held on to the trick of mentally switching channels, creating her own programs to block out troubling thoughts.

But this morning it seemed that her subconscious had appointed itself executive producer, forcing her to watch last night's love scenes over and over again. Could she really have been that woman, kneeling between that man's thighs, tasting every inch of his body with her lips?

Even as she struggled with disbelief, Lara felt the furnacelike heat generated by the masculine body that lay curled spoonlike against her backside.

How could she deny her wanton behavior of last night, when even now she could feel the weight of her breasts cradled against the hard calluses of a farmer's palm? Tanner's arms encircled her, one curving beneath her neck, the other draped across her midriff, his hands cupped to receive the soft caress of her nipples with each breath she took.

A small turn of her head pressed her ear flat against a wall of muscles sheathed in tight, leathery skin. Beneath that skin she could hear the steady thud of Tanner's heart, beating in rhythm with the warm breaths that gently brushed her cheek.

A slight shift of her lower body revealed a twinge of soreness between her thighs, caused, no doubt, by the bold shaft that even now was thrusting insistently into the wedge-shaped crevice between her buttocks. Evidently she wasn't the only one reliving last night.

Lara felt hot coals of embarrassment burning in her cheeks. She could just imagine what Tanner was thinking of her now. What on earth had possessed her last night?

She knew she was a passionate woman. Her marriage had taught her at least that much. But she had never behaved so wantonly, not even with Kevin. Her ex-husband had thought her oversexed, as it was.

There she had been, in front of a blazing fire, isolated by a winter storm—in the perfect romantic setting, except that she had been all alone. And it had been New Year's Eve. Was there anything more depressing than being alone and lonely on New Year's Eve?

During her marriage this holiday had been a private, intimate celebration. Kevin, normally an insatiable party-goer, had always preferred to leave the parties on "amateur night" to the rest of the population. Had they still been married, she would have spent a long, cozy evening in front of the fire, curled up with Kevin and a bottle of champagne.

She had set herself up, Lara realized. Determined not to spend another New Year's Eve questioning her decision to leave Kevin, she had created a head full of romantic fantasies. She would dance in the arms of a handsome, new man, surrounded by the voices and laughter of old friends. It was supposed to have been the best New Year's Eve ever, the perfect way to begin a year she hoped would bring the happiness and love she longed for.

All the daydreaming had made the cold reality of sitting home alone even more frigid. Not even the roaring fire had been able to thaw the atmosphere of bitter discontent.

Then the desires that had been kept dampened too long began to stretch hungrily toward the flames. No matter how many times she told herself she didn't have to have a man to be happy, there was always a little voice inside that whispered, *Liar.*

Maybe she didn't need a man to support her, but she desperately wanted one to hold and love her. Lying now in Tanner's embrace, she realized just how much she had missed the simple pleasure of waking up in a man's arms.

Last night she had given in to the sensuous fantasies aroused by her unsatisfied needs. She had indulged herself by creating a phantom lover in Tanner's image, never believing that the real thing would emerge from the violent winter storm.

As if to verify just how real he was, Tanner chose that moment to insinuate one hair-roughened thigh between her legs. One hand released its possessive hold on her breast and slid over her ribs, to rest lazily on the curve of her hip.

Lara held her breath and willed herself to lie still. *Please don't let him wake up yet*, she prayed silently. She had no idea how she was going to face him. Mornings after weren't in her range of expertise.

Beneath her ear the solid wall continued rising and falling in the rhythm of sleep. It seemed she was to be spared a while longer, but Lara realized the reprieve would be brief. Tanner was sure to wake up soon.

Tanner. She repeated his name in her thoughts. What had possessed him to struggle through the bitter cold just to reach her? No man took those kinds of risks just for a one-night stand. Kevin would never have taken such chances, and she was sure that he had loved her in his own way.

Lara winced. Did she have to keep coming back to Kevin? Was she forever bound to compare every man she met to her ex? Maybe it was inevitable. Theirs was the only serious relationship she had experienced.

There had been a few men of interest since her divorce, but none had sparked the same, instinctive recognition she had felt with Kevin. None till Tanner. Was that what had made her respond to him that night at the Jube?

Driving a strange drunk home had certainly been out of character for her. Oh, she would never let someone who had overindulged drive, but in Houston she would simply have called a cab for him. Of course, there weren't any cabs in Morristown, but she could have let one of the boys drive him home, at least let Kelly or Susan follow them.

Why had she become so determined to take care of him, so sure that she was the only one who could?

Destiny wasn't so difficult to believe, when she looked back over her brief romantic history. The one time she had let a man take her home on the first date had resulted in marriage. What were the odds against its happening a second time?

She was certain that Kevin, with his rakish past, had never anticipated marrying the young virgin he'd met in a dusty, law firm's filing room.

Was it destiny that had scattered a few, special men in her path, leaving them as stepping-stones from the innocence of youth to the distant bank, where "happily ever after" waited?

She had thought she had reached the other side safely when she married Kevin. But he had proven to be only an island in the stream. Evidently her crossing wasn't meant to be that easy. Now the stones seemed farther apart, and the current flowed faster and faster between them.

Was Tanner the destination or just another stone?

As the man in question tightened his grasp on her, Lara once more held her breath and waited. She was going to find out the answer all too soon. Even now she could feel his body hardening with early-morning arousal.

Desperate, she closed her eyes and fought her body's instinctive response. Forcing herself to lie still as she felt him stir beside her, she waited cautiously to see which way the current was running before jumping in.

It was a shame, she decided, that her legal training hadn't taught her how to think as swiftly off her feet as on them.

Awareness of Lara's soft, warm body nestled snugly against his own gradually seeped into Tanner's mind, coaxing him to abandon his dreams for an even sweeter reality.

He remembered clearly the moment he had looked through the window, seeing Lara on the hearth, idly feeding the fire. He'd wanted her so badly, but had been unable to reach her through the glass.

How many times had he dreamed of Jodi, of fighting all odds to reach her, only to find that she was always beyond his grasp? No matter how close he came, Jodi always took another step, traveling farther and farther away.

But Lara had walked toward him. She had opened the door and taken him into her arms. Somehow she had banished all thoughts of Jodi. Tanner had never dreamed of finding a woman capable of that.

Last night, thinking of anyone but Lara had been impossible. Thinking of anything had been impossible. His mind had been stormed, first by the need and then the satisfaction of all his desires.

Once more he could feel her lips on his body, her hands stroking every inch of his muscular frame.

Lara had made love to him.

He had never known what it could be like to have a woman make love to him, with him, instead of just allowing him to make love to her. Until Lara he had never understood that there was a difference. Now he knew— and had an overwhelming desire to experience it again.

In the faint, blue light of morning, Tanner let his eyes slowly drift over Lara's sleeping form. Carefully he studied each feature, each curve and then placed the vision in his mind beside the memories of last night.

His right hand began to wander, sliding softly over her silken skin. There had been no time last night for comparisons, but now it occurred to him how utterly different two women could be physically. It had seemed that while trying to blot out Jodi's memory, he had constantly discovered her clone. But Lara was nothing like Jodi.

Her breasts were rounder, fuller. Her hips were wider, contrasting nicely with her trim waist. Her legs were shorter, more curvaceous. Lara left an impression of substance, the overall package more compact. Her full figure promised the warmth and comfort that Tanner craved.

Jodi had had an ethereal quality that extended from her physique to her vagrant life-style. She was a will-o'-the-wisp who'd always managed to escape him, no matter how tightly he had tried to hold on.

Gently Tanner eased away from Lara, just enough to lower her onto her back for a more thorough exploration. His movements became more urgent as he felt his hunger return in full force, oblivious to the satisfaction he had experienced last night.

As he lowered his head to blaze a trail of kisses along her neck, he let his hand slide forward over her hip, feeling the slight rise of her abdomen against his palm. Here, too, Lara was fuller. He recalled vividly the taut, almost concave curve of Jodi's body. Slowly he began to caress Lara's belly, delighting in her soft shape.

Lara moaned out loud before she could stop herself.

Tanner halted his hand instantly. "Lara? What's wrong? Did I hurt you?"

Reluctantly she lifted long, sandy lashes and stared into dark golden eyes filled with concern. "You don't have to rub it in."

Tanner stared at her blankly. "I don't understand. What's wrong?"

Sighing heavily, she grasped his large hand with both of hers and removed it from her least favorite attribute. "I'm fat. That's what's wrong. And massaging it doesn't make it go away. Nothing does."

Tanner grinned at her disgruntled expression. Pulling his hand out of her grasp, he returned it to the offending portion of her anatomy. "You mean this little curve here?"

"A gentleman would overlook it," she said in a stern voice. She lowered her hands to remove his again, but Tanner ignored her efforts to shoo him away. His deep laugh rumbled through the quiet as he gently began to knead her soft belly with his fingers.

"No man, gentleman or not, would overlook such a thing of beauty."

"It's not beauty. It's fat and I hate it. I can still remember Grandma Hess patting my stomach and saying, 'You're just a fat little pig, aren't you?'"

Tanner laughed. "If your grandmother was a Hess, she must have been German. She probably meant it as a compliment. German men like their women with a little meat on their bones." Lowering his head, he nipped her earlobe with strong, white teeth, then whispered intimately, "So do Scots."

Lara tilted her head back, allowing him access to the soft, white curve of her neck. "Do they really?"

"Mmm-hmm." Tanner nibbled his way along her jawline, slowly making his way toward her pouting lips. "Especially this one."

Lara was still doubtful, but was willing to be convinced. She met his kiss eagerly, her misgivings about last night forgotten for the moment. Who could argue with a man who liked potbellies?

She stretched lazily, arching her back as Tanner's fingers finally decided to continue their search even lower. When their journey revealed the moistness already waiting for him between her legs, he smiled with the anticipation every great explorer must have felt at the moment of discovery.

As he moved to cover her body, Lara automatically parted her thighs to admit him, wrapping her legs around his strong, lean hips. Even as his lips met hers in a gentle, searching kiss, she could feel the pulsating length of his manhood poised to enter her.

"Mmm," she moaned against his mouth. "Do you always wake up feeling like this?"

Tanner shook his head, letting his mouth brush across hers. "No, but I think it might become a habit, if I keep letting you tuck me in at night."

Lara smiled wickedly. "Now that sounds like a New Year's resolution worth keeping. I resolve to do everything within my power to see that Tanner McNeil wakes up . . . smiling."

"This is one New Year's resolution I am going to hold you to," Tanner promised.

"Please do," she whispered huskily. "Hold me tight, Tanner."

He obliged without hesitation, tightening his grasp on her hips as he slipped smoothly inside. Throughout the long winter's night their bodies had established an intimate rapport. Now they fitted together effortlessly, each moving and bending to accommodate the other.

"Oh, Tanner. You feel so good."

"So do you, baby. So do you."

She arched her body again, allowing Tanner to deepen his penetration. It was slow, tortuous love-making, each teasing the other until neither could bear it any longer. Lara slid her hands down his sweat-slicked back, then grasped his hips and pulled him hard against her, forcing him first to quicken the pace before she matched his rhythm with her own movements.

The seductive whispering and laughing innuendos were heard no longer, leaving a silence filled only with the sounds of two bodies desperately trying to merge beyond the limits of human physiology.

Lara felt Tanner stiffen and shuddered herself as the tide of passion finally overcame them, crashing furiously against the barrier of nerves and flesh, before it slid into the gentle ebb of total satisfaction.

Sated for the moment, each gulped for the air their lungs had been denied in the struggle for completion. Tanner let his body collapse against Lara's, knowing that he was too heavy, but unable to support his own weight on his weakened limbs.

"Never, Lara. It's never been like that with anyone else."

"Not for me, either."

Tanner mustered what strength he had left, raising his head to study her. "Not even with Kevin?"

Lara let her eyes meet his, let him see the truth she knew was there. "Not with anyone. Not even Kevin."

Tanner released a rush of air. Leaning forward, he brushed a light kiss across her lips, before rolling slowly off her body to lie beside her, one leg still lying across her thighs. A hand remained, possessively covering the slight rise of her belly.

"I'm glad it wasn't like this with him," he said honestly. "I want everything about us to be special. Unique between us."

"It is, Tanner. It is. Kevin would never have taken the risks you did last night to get here. I still can't believe that you did. When I woke up this morning, I half expected that you had just been a figment of my imagination."

His brow arched in curiosity. "Oh, really? Just what have you been imagining?"

Lara flushed uncomfortably. "Never mind. I just meant that, well . . ." She stumbled over the words, knowing that no matter how intimate she had just been with this man, she wasn't about to tell her fantasies to anyone.

But Tanner refused to let her off so easily. "Now that you mention it, you didn't seem at all surprised to see me at your window last night. Were you thinking about me . . . about us? Were you imagining how good we could be together?"

Tanner nuzzled the soft skin behind her ear as he spoke, then punctuated his questions with sharp little nibbles on her earlobe. "Was that what you imagined Lara? Me and you in front of the fire, our bodies locked together, making love?"

Lara felt the shimmers racing down her spine in response to his soft murmurings. "Tanner," she said, speaking his name in a weak protest.

Gently he pressed her back against the mattress. Holding her still with one hand planted squarely on her middle, he used the other to tilt up her chin, forcing her to witness the passion he knew was etched on his face.

"Don't be embarrassed, Lara. That's what I imagined. That's what drove me here last night. All I could think of was you, here, waiting for me." Then he smiled and shook his head, laughing wryly at himself. "I have to admit, though, my imagination was pretty poor compared to the real thing. My wildest fantasies seem tame after last night."

"You must think I'm some kind of wild woman," Lara groaned.

"My kind of wild woman. An endangered species, and it's my responsibility to see that you're protected from poachers and predators." Tanner sighed. "It's a tough job, but someone's got to do it."

She tentatively lifted a hand to trace the strong, chiseled planes of his face. "Are you sure you want to take on that kind of responsibility?"

"I'd like to see someone stop me." The grin he had been wearing disappeared, and his muscles tensed as his body prepared to defend his right to be her protector. "I may be a little slow sometimes—"

"Really?" she interrupted. "I hadn't noticed."

He frowned discouragingly. "I may have been a little slow about seeing the light with Jodi," he continued, "but I'm not making any mistakes with you."

"No morning-after regrets?" she suggested.

"No!" He was obviously shocked that she would even think there could be.

Lara smiled at his vehement response. "It was pretty special, wasn't it?"

"Very special," he agreed, placing a brief kiss on the soft pad of her thumb as it smoothed the firm curves of his mouth.

She licked her lips delicately. "Do you believe in fate, Tanner?"

"Did you ever meet a farmer who didn't?"

"No," she admitted, "I haven't. I was just thinking that maybe we were destined to be together last night."

Tanner nodded. "No 'maybe' about it. We were destined to be together. Last night. Next week. Next year. Forever and ever. Amen."

Only then did Lara realize how anxious she had been about the future of this newborn relationship. But she needn't have worried about Tanner's intentions. He had already foreseen a future, light-years ahead of her own expectations.

"And with any luck," he added huskily, "maybe another destiny began to take shape last night, as well."

Lara knew an unasked question lurked behind his words, but couldn't fathom what he meant. Her eyes met his, silently asking for clarification. But Tanner suddenly seemed reluctant to speak.

Instead he let his eyes slide down her body, skimming over her breasts and midriff before coming to a halt where his hand lay on the curved plane between her hipbones, fingers spread to encompass the smooth surface of her skin.

She followed his visual trail with her own eyes, and blushed uncomfortably when she came to the end. It was nice to find a man who didn't pat her belly and then suggest she start doing a few more sit-ups, but she would have preferred he overlook her obvious flaw altogether.

Flushing uncomfortably, she felt him staring once more at her face, clearly searching for some response. Still she couldn't discern what he meant. Then he lightly squeezed the fingers covering her womb and Lara knew instantly what he was asking.

"No!"

Tanner recoiled automatically from the force of her denial.

Lara laughed shakily. "Sorry, I didn't mean to yell. It's not a problem, though. I mean, you don't have to worry." She'd intended to reassure him, but Tanner didn't look relieved. In fact, just the opposite. She would swear he was actually disappointed.

"Are you sure, honey?"

"Tanner..." She hesitated briefly, her hand reaching out to grasp his as it now hovered above her skin. "Tanner, I'm on the pill. I started taking them when I got married and have taken them ever since. There's no way I'm pregnant. Don't worry."

He pulled away from her, swinging his legs over the other side of the bed to sit on the edge with his back toward her. "I wasn't exactly worried to start with."

She moved with him, rising on her knees behind him, sliding her hands over the heavily muscled contours of his back. "Tanner, you are supposed to be relieved. What's wrong?"

"I thought you wanted kids. Isn't that one of the reasons you left your ex-husband?"

"Well, yes, but I don't want them as a result of a one-night stand. No matter how good it was."

Tanner whirled around abruptly, sending Lara tumbling back against the mattress. "Who said anything about a one-night stand?" he asked angrily.

Lara scooted backward, retreating from the anger that flashed in his eyes. "I just meant that one night in bed doesn't make a relationship," she said, adopting the calm, rational voice she used for soothing irate, irrational clients.

He shook his head, leaning forward to plant a fist on either side of her body. "I thought we just agreed that we were destined to be together. Destiny doesn't fool around with one-night stands. It only messes with the real thing."

"But don't you think it's a little too soon to be sure of that, Tanner? We barely know each other. It was really too soon for us to go to bed together, much less make a baby. Be reasonable."

"Too soon? Why?" he asked. "We're both committed to building a life in Morristown. We both want to get married and create a home. We both want a family, and we're fantastic in bed together."

"We've also both been burned badly by past relationships," she added.

"So?"

"So it takes time to get over that," she explained patiently.

"Are you still in love with Kevin, then? Is that what you're saying?" Tanner spoke harshly, his jaw clenched.

"No, that's not what I'm saying. But even after two years of being divorced, I know that my marriage and divorce are still coloring my relationships." Lara pressed her hands against his broad chest, firmly pushing him back so that she could sit up and face him squarely.

"I don't want to make another mistake, Tanner. Divorce was hard enough when it only affected me. I would hate to put a child through that. I won't put my child through that."

Tanner felt his anger slip away. "It wouldn't be a mistake. I'm sure of that."

"As sure as you used to be about Jodi?"

She might as well have slapped him across the face. Pain clouded his eyes, and Lara knew that she had cut him to the quick. But sometimes a slap was just what was needed to bring a person back to his senses.

When he would have pulled away again, Lara stopped him, clutching his upper arms with all her strength. "I'm sorry, Tanner. Believe me, I understand what you're going through. But creating a child and getting married on the rebound aren't the answer. It wouldn't be fair to you or me and certainly wouldn't be fair to a child."

"I'm not on the rebound."

"Then there's no hurry."

"I'm supposed to spend the rest of my life alone, because I screwed up one time?"

"No," Lara answered firmly, "but you do give yourself time to get over the bitterness, so that it doesn't affect your chance for happiness in the future."

"And how long am I supposed to allow, Lara? Is there some magic incubation period? Damn it, I waited seven years for Jodi to change before giving up. Am I supposed to wait another seven years to be sure I'm over her, before I can settle down with you? Assuming you would wait that long. I'm thirty-two now. I don't want to wait till I'm forty to have a family."

Lara pressed down harder on his arms. "I'm not saying that you have to wait seven years, or even one year. I'm just saying slow down. Give us time to really get to know each other. Give yourself time to resolve your feelings for Jodi."

Tanner shook his head stubbornly. "I don't need time. But if you need it, I'll give it to you. Just don't ask me to be too patient, Lara. My patience has just about reached its limit."

Exhaustion seeped in as their overwrought emotions drained away, taking what was left of their energy. Lara released Tanner, and he lay back against the pillows, pulling her down, so that her head rested in the hollow of one broad shoulder.

"If destiny really did intend for us to be together, it will all work out, Tanner. Just relax, okay?"

He shook his head against the pillow. "I'll relax when you quit worrying about other people, who don't mean anything to either of us anymore."

5

THE BLIZZARD FINALLY blew itself out around 3:00 a.m. the next morning. January 1 dawned bright and clear, gleaming with perfection as the sun's rays bounced off a pristine, white blanket.

Soon, however, the smooth coverlet was marred by footsteps, sled runners, tire tracks and snow angels as the citizens of Morristown rushed out to enjoy the snow, secure in the knowledge that it would not stay for long.

Lara had driven Tanner outside, hoping the chill in the air would cool the emotional intensity between them. But he had turned the plan against her, using the winter magic to weave an even tighter spell of intimacy about them.

The day could have made a scene in an old MGM musical, the snow providing the perfect backdrop. Of course, Tanner was cast as the leading man, but what role would she play? Lara wondered. The star-struck ingenue or the sadder-but-wiser girl?

The script came straight from the lyrics of "Walking in a Winter Wonderland," and Tanner had done his best to bring the song to life with his booming voice. He had even insisted on dubbing their chubby snowman Parson Brown.

Later, frozen from head to toe, they had stumbled back inside to cuddle in front of the fire, alternately

feeding each other popcorn between sips of hot chocolate.

When Lara finally forced Tanner to go home on the
morning of the second, the snow had already been
transformed from the crisp whiteness of a new baby's
blanket to the dingy scrap of a toddler's "blanky." By
the fifth, all that was left of the storm was a few scattered snow people, slowly sinking into the front yards
where they had stood.

Even the "parson" had become scandalously tipsy,
before succumbing to the heat of the sun and disap-
pearing altogether. The possibility that Tanner's interest might melt just as fast loomed ominously in Lara's
mind.

But it hadn't yet. In fact it seemed to be gathering
speed like a giant snowball rolling down a steep hill.
The morning after New Year's she had forced him away,
and knew that she'd only succeeded because they both
had work to do.

That evening, and every evening since, she had
waited in front of the fire, torn between the fear and the
hope of falling in love. She promised herself that tonight—if there was a tonight—she would force them
back to some form of normality. But her good intentions were always swept away by the shivers that shot
down her spine warning her, assuring her that he had
come back again.

Mindful of curious neighbors and the ever-present,
small-town communications network, Tanner always
parked his truck at the bottom of the hill, hiding it
among the trees. Then he would walk up through the
woods to wait outside the French doors.

From that moment until the first streak of color pierced the navy-blue darkness just before dawn, they would be caught up in a reenactment of New Year's Eve. It was a scene from a classic, Lara thought—she knew all the lines by heart, but even after watching it a thousand times, it still brought tears to her eyes.

She still couldn't completely dispel the notion that he was a fantasy lover conjured up from the fire by her imagination. Perhaps that was why she had allowed their relationship to continue raging out of control. If it wasn't real, how could she get burned?

ON FEBRUARY 14th, Cupid found Lara sitting at her desk, twisting the blood-red rose in her fingers, while studying a gnarly root with short, barren branches that lay on her desk. The flower and the stick plant, which she believed had once been a rosebush, had been lying on the front steps when she arrived at work that morning.

There was no card and no explanation. Though she knew somehow who they were from, she didn't have a clue as to what either meant.

Closing her eyes briefly, she allowed herself to drift into warm thoughts of Tanner. It had felt so good to be held again, to relax in the luxury of simple companionship. It had been so hard for her to send him home this morning.

She was beginning to believe that something so good couldn't be a mistake. Maybe Tanner was right; they both wanted the same things out of life, and that alone gave them more in common than she and Kevin had ever had.

She smiled, remembering his surprise when she told him that tonight he must come to the front door. Tonight would be the perfect time to start finding out if they did have a chance together.

A determined buzzing finally penetrated her thoughts, and Lara realized that the receptionist had been trying to get her attention for several seconds. Pressing the intercom button, she answered, "Yes, Karen?"

"Susan Metcalf is here. She doesn't have an appointment, but she said it was important that she see you."

"I'll be right out." Lara shoved thoughts of her love life aside, hid the flower and stick plant beneath her desk and went to meet her friend and client.

Susan's divorce was still a few weeks away from being final, but Lara thought everything had been taken care of except the formalities. Shrugging into her suit jacket, she walked toward the reception area she shared with Bill Harris.

"Susan, how are you? I see you survived the holidays."

The attractive, but weary-looking newspaper editor stepped forward swiftly to accept Lara's hand. "I'm sorry to bother you. I know I should have called first."

"Nonsense," Lara assured her. "Come on back, so we can talk."

Susan hesitated, seeming reluctant to enter the private office.

"Come on in and have a seat," Lara invited her friend again. "I'll pour you some coffee and we'll have a nice visit." She tried her best to put her friend at ease, but Susan still seemed terribly distressed. Lara had an uneasy feeling and hoped that for once her instincts were wrong.

"No coffee, thanks. I don't want to take up any more of your time than necessary." Susan twisted her hands in her lap, sitting on the very edge of her chair.

"Don't be silly. I'm your friend as well as your attorney. What's wrong? Has Hank been bothering you or the kids?"

"No. That is, not exactly." Susan's gaze traveled somewhat desperately over the room, as though searching for something to focus on besides Lara. Finally she lowered her eyes and spoke while looking at her lap.

"I know you'll think I'm foolish, but I've decided to take Hank back. He came over on Christmas Eve and helped me put the kids' presents under the tree. It was almost like old times. We talked for hours. He's come back several times since and, well, he says he's sorry and it won't ever happen again." She raised her eyes to see Lara's worried expression. "I believe him, Lara. Honest I do."

"Maybe he does mean it now, Susan, but that's no guarantee for good behavior in the future."

"He said he'd try," Susan murmured. "Hank really isn't a bad man. I know that's probably hard for you to believe, after all the awful things I said about him, but they were really just angry words. I was hurt by what he did."

"I know you were hurt," Lara agreed. "That is why I'm worried about this decision. I don't want to see you hurt again, Susan."

"I appreciate that, but I really think it's for the best. The kids miss him, and we would be a lot better off financially if we stayed together."

"Is that what really made you change your mind?" Lara asked gently. "Are you afraid you won't be able to make it on your own?"

"It wouldn't be easy," Susan admitted. "I still need to put most of the profits back into the newspaper. So much of the equipment needs to be updated, not to mention hiring more staff."

"What about the house? I thought you were going to sell it and move in with your parents. Won't that help?"

"Yes, but . . ." Susan shook her head, then looked directly into Lara's eyes. "You're a damn good attorney, Lara. And I know that you're speaking as a lawyer right now. But as my friend, can you honestly tell me you've never regretted leaving your husband? That you don't worry about being alone for the rest of your life? That's what I am really afraid of. Hank may not be perfect, but he is mine. What are the odds that I'll find another man here in Morristown?"

"Okay, maybe the selection here is limited, but there are still men here. Kelly always seems to find a date."

"A date, yes, but a husband? And what about you? How many dates have you had since you've been back?"

"A few."

"Any with potential?"

"Maybe," Lara hedged.

"So you've been holding out on us, hmm? Who is it—? No, wait. Let me guess. Tanner McNeil."

Lara nodded reluctantly.

"That just proves my point," Susan said. "What man is going to be attracted to me—a woman with a ready-made family and a struggling business—when he's got two gorgeous women to choose from who don't have any encumbrances?"

"I think you're selling the men here short. You're an attractive, intelligent, successful woman with two wonderful kids. Why shouldn't they be interested in you?"

"Well, I've been separated for six months, and I haven't had anyone beating down my door yet."

"Susan . . ."

"No, Lara. I'm sorry, but I have to give Hank one more chance. We've been together too long to just throw it all away now."

"It's your decision, Susan, but I wish you would think it over some more. There have been times when I've wondered if I should have stayed with Kevin, but basically I know I made the right decision."

"And you aren't afraid of spending the rest of your life alone?"

"Afraid? No, I'm not afraid. It would not be my first choice, but I could live with it. Happily." Lara meant what she said, but she could see Susan was doubtful.

Gently she added, "Staying married to Hank doesn't mean you won't be left alone, Susan. Life doesn't give us those kinds of guarantees. Whether he's in a car wreck tomorrow or just out painting the town, you'll still be by yourself. Think about it."

Susan shrugged wearily. "I have thought about it, Lara. Filing for the divorce really shook Hank up. He knows I won't stand for any more dallying around. Maybe knowing I had the guts to leave him made him respect me more. Anyway, I have to give him another chance. For the children's sake, if nothing else. When you have kids of your own, you'll understand."

"I understand now. But playing devil's advocate is part of my job. Look, if you want to give Hank another chance, fine. I can postpone the final proceedings for a while. Has he already moved back in?"

Susan shook her head. "Not yet. I told him I needed time to think it over." She hesitated a moment, then admitted guiltily, "I didn't want him to think I've just been sitting around, pining for him."

"Good," Lara said. "Then you are still legally separated. You could just date each other for a while, without affecting the status of the proceedings. If things don't work out, it will save you the time and cost of having to go through the separation period again and refiling all the papers."

"But why should we date, when we're already married? What is the point?"

"The point is that you have already proven you are strong enough to leave him. It's his turn to prove that he is worth coming back to. Give yourself some time to be sure he's going to keep those promises."

"I don't know."

Sensing her friend's doubt, Lara put her finely honed persuasive skills to work. "Look, you were married right out of high school. You've never really had a chance to date as an adult. If nothing else, this will give you the opportunity to put a little romance back in your relationship."

"Well, maybe."

"And as long as you are back in the dating game, you might as well date a few other men, too."

"Now wait a second, Lara!" Susan jumped up. "How am I supposed to get my marriage back together, if I'm seeing other men? Hank will never go for that."

"It will be his loss." Lara the lawyer was hitting her stride now. "As long as you're separated, I think you owe it to yourself to look at all your options. It's a mistake to go back to Hank, only because you're afraid of alternatives you haven't even explored yet."

"And if I did want to do some exploring, who am I supposed to do it with? Like I said, no one has been beating down my door these past few months."

"Don't worry. Between me, Kelly and Tanner, I'm sure we will have plenty of candidates for you to choose from. All you have to do is agree to go out with them."

Susan stood shaking her head.

"Look," Lara hurried on, not wanting to lose the advantage, "you have already told Hank you need some time to think it over. All I'm asking is that you go ahead and push for an extension of that time. If he really wants you back, he shouldn't have any problem with that."

"And what if during this extension he discovers that he really doesn't want me back?"

There was no snappy reply this time. Instead Lara spoke softly and in all seriousness. "Then you will be a lot better off than if he had discovered it after you had already gotten back together."

Susan turned to stare out the window, while Lara stood quietly in the background, knowing that she had said enough. She hoped she hadn't let her tongue go too far.

"Have I told you how glad I am that you're back?"

The voice came out so small, Lara wasn't sure at first if Susan had actually spoken. Then her client turned around and walked toward her with the threat of tears in her eyes.

» "And have I told you how much it means to have an attorney who is such a good friend?"

Smiling tremulously, Lara gladly accepted the warm hug she was offered. "It's mutual. I am very picky about my clients." She hesitated briefly, then proceeded like the good lawyer she knew she was. "I will file for a postponement, tomorrow. Okay? You can tell Hank he has six months to redeem himself."

"It's a deal. Thanks, Lara."

"Hey, that's what lawyers are for. We're really just a bunch of Dear Abby's who charge by the hour."

Susan laughed for the first time in days. "Now you tell me. I should have hired you as a columnist instead of an attorney."

They were both laughing as Lara walked her to her car.

Just before Susan pulled away, Lara reminded her. "Now don't forget, when Kelly and I set you up with someone, you're going to say yes."

"You mean when they ask me out?"

"Then, too."

"Lara!" Susan exclaimed.

Lara was still grinning like a Cheshire cat when she closed the front door.

Sometimes her job could be terribly depressing. Seeing families break up, even when it was for the best, was never easy. But on days like today, when she was sure she had helped someone make the right decision... Well, for her, that was what being a lawyer was all about.

And traumatic though it had been for her emotionally, she knew her own divorce had made her better professionally. She *did* understand Susan's change of heart. Leaving her own marriage had been scary, and she hadn't had children to worry about. Of course, if she'd had children, she might not have felt the need to leave in the first place.

It all seemed such a terrible maze. She had left her husband because she'd wanted a family, and now she faced the very real possibility that she would have to spend the rest of her life with neither a man nor a child. Susan's second thoughts were easy to understand.

Against her will, the memory of begging Kevin to take her back flashed across her mind in full Technicolor. Could anything have been more humiliating? At least Susan had been spared that.

To give him credit, Kevin hadn't taken full advantage of the moment. Nevertheless, his rejection had cut deep, as deep as her leaving had probably hurt him.

Tit for tat. That was what equality had come to mean to them. The ideal marriage of equals had become a war zone, where each gave as good as they got. And as in any war, there had been no true winner.

Her analytical brain had studied and dissected every aspect of her marriage—too much, she admitted. And she was starting to do the same thing with Tanner. Sometimes she wished she could just turn off her brain and go with the flow. Self-analysis, she decided, was the intelligent woman's guide to masochism.

Lord, she thought, *I've got to quit thinking like this.* Grabbing her briefcase and her purse, she prepared to leave. She still had a couple of hours before Tanner was due to arrive for dinner. Just enough time to take a long, hot soak while the roast simmered in the oven.

She had planned a full-course meal. When she had pushed Tanner out the door this morning, she had given

him strict instructions not to appear before seven
o'clock and to please bring a bottle of wine to go with
dinner, not so subtly letting him know that she wasn't
going to be rushed off to bed this time.

Lara made it to the front door of the building before
she remembered the rose and the stick plant. Slowly she
walked back to her office and retrieved the mysterious
gifts. What the hell did they mean? As she stared at the
barren plant, it occurred to her that all her planning for
tonight might have been totally unnecessary. Maybe
this was Tanner's way of saying their romance was
dead.

But then why include the bloom? A single rose tra-
ditionally meant "I love you." But what did a dead
rosebush mean?

WHEN HER DOORBELL RANG two hours later, Lara was
still puzzling over her mysterious Valentine. Startled,
she glanced at the clock on her nightstand, which confirmed that her caller must be Tanner. Right on time.
Damn, why couldn't he have been running late, too?

Quickly pulling the edges of her robe together, she
hurried downstairs to answer the door. At least the
message he had left that morning hadn't meant goodbye, she reassured herself.

Her city habits refused to die easily, she reflected, as
she found herself standing on tiptoe to look out the
peephole. The warped viewpoint did nothing to di-
minish the impact of Tanner's handsome profile, nor
could it disguise the surprisingly formal suit he was
wearing.

Lara's heart quickened at the very sight of him. She
felt the dampness of her palms against the cold, metal

doorknob and realized suddenly that if she opened the door now, in her half-naked state, all her plans for this evening would be history.

After sliding the safety chain into place, she opened the door a crack, bracing her body against the slab of wood. She saw Tanner instantly start forward, only to come to an abrupt halt when it became apparent the door was not going to open any farther.

"Lara, what's wrong? Open up."

Peering around the edge of the door, Lara shook her head. "Sorry, Tanner, but you can't come in yet. It'll just take me a few more minutes to finish dressing. I'll let you in then."

"Sounds like a waste of time to me. Why don't you let me in now and I'll get undressed? Then we can both be comfortable." Tanner stepped forward again as he spoke, pressing against the door. The chain stretched taut, but held, drawing his attention.

"Did I do something wrong? Has something happened?" he asked, confused by her action. "Surely you're not afraid of me, Lara?"

"Of course not," she assured him. "But I'm not a fool, either. I told you tonight was going to be different. I've had enough of the clandestine rendezvous with you sneaking in and out of my bedroom. If we are going to have a relationship, we are going to back up and do it right. That means a candlelit dinner and conversation, not just sex."

"Fine, I'm kind of hungry myself," Tanner agreed easily. "Let me in and we'll eat. There's still no point in my waiting for you to get dressed up. After all, it isn't like we're going out to some fancy restaurant." He pushed on the door once more, but both the chain and Lara refused to budge.

"You're dressed up," she pointed out.

"Only because I had meetings with the bank in Jonesboro today. I didn't make it back in time to go home and change. Believe me, I intend to ditch this monkey suit as soon as I get inside."

"Sorry," Lara repeated. "You are just going to have to wait out there until I'm dressed. And I don't think it will hurt you to wear the monkey suit a little longer. You look very handsome in it. Perfect for a Valentine's dinner."

"Fine. I'll keep it on. Why don't you let me in and I can help you with zippers and things?"

"Fat chance. I know you better than that, Tanner McNeil. As far as you're concerned, zippers only go one way, and it isn't up."

He grinned wickedly, not even bothering to deny the allegation. During the past few weeks he had managed to make her late for the office several times by "helping" her get dressed. He would have felt guilty about it, if it hadn't been obvious that she worked too hard, anyway. He didn't see the point of being your own boss, if you couldn't be a little late once in a while.

"You'll just have to wait out there until I'm ready," she said again.

"But, Lara, it's cold out here."

"Good. You could use a little cooling off."

"It's not that cold."

"Then it won't hurt you to wait. I'll let you in as soon as I'm ready." Shutting the door on his protests, she locked it securely before scurrying up the stairs to finish dressing.

Tossing her robe onto the bed, she quickly slipped into the lacy, black underwear she had already laid out, then slid silk stockings up her legs and secured them to her garter belt.

Reaching into her closet, she pulled out her favorite, little black dress and had tugged the zipper halfway up before she remembered the exchange with Tanner. It would take him about two seconds to get her out of this dress. Tempting, but definitely not part of tonight's plan. Reluctantly she put the dress back and searched through her wardrobe for something safer. She finally found the perfect answer in an emerald wool-jersey dress with fifty *faux* pearl buttons marching up the front. Perfect.

She only unfastened a few at the top to pull it over her head, but she would make sure that Tanner undid every single one before she let him take it off later. Just the sight of so many delicate buttons should be enough to intimidate a man with hands as large as his.

Sliding her feet into matching pumps, she walked to the three-way mirror that stood in the corner of the dressing area she had once shared with her two older sisters. Turning slightly, she checked her image from all sides.

One hand on the curve of her abdomen, she debated exchanging the stockings and garter belt for control-top panty hose. She decided against it. Tanner swore he found the soft curve appealing, so who was she to argue with him?

At that moment the doorbell rang again, indicating the man in question was tired of cooling his heels. Taking a deep breath to steady her nerves, Lara walked downstairs to greet her guest once more.

She fumbled as she undid the chain, telling herself it was silly to feel this jittery. She had lost count of the number of times she and Tanner had made love, and yet here she was, as nervous as a teenager going on her first date.

But this would be their first date in many ways, she reminded herself. A few jitters were only natural. Taking one more deep breath, she opened the door.

Tanner stood transfixed for a moment, his hand poised above the bell, obviously ready to ring it again. Looking dazed, he let his arm drop back to his side as he walked through the entrance, not once taking his eyes off Lara.

"You look beautiful," he whispered hoarsely as he came to a stop in front of her.

"Worth waiting for?"

"Definitely." His eyes traveled over her thoroughly, narrowing slightly as he took in the row of buttons. He frowned for just a moment, then the sexy smile came back stronger than ever. Clearly he was undaunted by the thought of fumbling through so many fastenings.

"I should warn you, I think," Tanner said.

Lara's eyes widened in surprise. "Warn me? About what?"

"Wrapping my presents. I'm the sort who undoes every piece of tape without tearing the paper."

"Oh, really?" She felt her mouth go dry, and her tongue slipped out to moisten her lips. "I'm the rip-it-open-tear-the-package-type myself."

"Mmm. I prefer to draw it out. Anticipation is part of the pleasure, sometimes the best part. Why hurry through it?"

"Then you should really enjoy tonight," Lara told him. "This evening we are going to take our time and have a real date. I've been much too easy thus far."

"You've been perfect."

Lara shivered uncontrollably at the impact of his husky words. What was it about this man that kept her so spellbound? He was too big and solid to be a dream. Even standing three feet away, she could feel the heat of his body reaching out to her.

He lifted one hand, gently trailing a finger down the row of buttons. "Are you really going to insist on dinner first?" he asked.

Shaking herself back to the present, Lara felt her feminine pride stiffen at his arrogance. "I am definitely going to insist on dinner. Whether it is first depends on whether I decide there will be anything after."

Tanner winced at her threat. "Are you amenable to bribery?"

"That depends on what you are offering."

For an answer Tanner opened the front door again and reached just outside for the bottle of wine he had left to chill in the cold air. Recognizing the label of an Arkansas winery, Lara smiled. The wine was almost impossible to find outside the state, and it was one of her favorites.

"Not bad," she admitted, then added, "for a start," before he could get too cocky.

"I thought you might like it," Tanner said with a nonchalance he certainly didn't feel. What he knew about wine would fit on the label Lara was admiring. Buying the Arkansas vintage had seemed the safest choice. He figured that anything grown in his home state couldn't be too bad.

"And it should be chilled just enough," Lara said.

"You're lucky it isn't frozen solid," he grumbled.

She laughed easily, refusing to feel any sympathy for him. Spinning on her heel, she marched into the kitchen, issuing an invitation for him to follow only as an afterthought.

"Come on, I'll let you do the honors with the wine while I finish getting dinner ready."

Tanner swallowed his nervousness and accepted the corkscrew, determined not to show his inexperience with the utensil. Turning his back to Lara, he fumbled silently, relaxing only when she became busy with the roast and, he hoped, was ignoring his efforts.

Fortunately the cork cooperated, coming out fairly easily and in one piece. Following his chef's orders, Tanner poured a little into the two glasses she provided, then nestled the bottle in the wine chiller.

"All set?" Lara asked.

Tanner nodded, lifting the tray bearing the wine and glasses as evidence. "Whenever you are."

"Right this way then." Carrying the platter with the roast and vegetables in one hand and a basket of bread in the other, Lara led him into the den, where she had set a service for two on the coffee table in front of the fire.

The table was pulled out to allow just enough room for them both to sit behind it, with the couch providing support for their backs. The electric lights were all out, but the fire Lara had built earlier provided a pleasant glow, aided by the candles she lighted as they sat down.

The conversation was put on hold as they ate, letting the saxophone that whispered seductively from the stereo fill the intimate silence.

"I hope you don't mind sitting on the floor," Lara said when the quiet intensity became more than she could endure. "I thought it would be a little cozier in here. The dining room is much too big for just two people."

"No problem," Tanner assured her. "In fact, I think this is very appropriate. Returning to the scene of the crime, so to speak."

"The crime?"

"Uh-huh, the crime of passion. Where it all began, one dark and stormy winter night."

It was too dark for Tanner to see if she was blushing, but from the way she was busying herself with tidying the table, he felt it safe to assume she was. "Quite appropriate, wouldn't you say?"

"Well, that might be a bit dramatic. I just thought we would be more comfortable here by the fire."

"You mean more intimate, don't you? Wasn't that what you promised me this morning? A romantic dinner for two with intimate conversation?" Tanner reached out to brush the rose, which now occupied a crystal bud vase in the center of the table. "Nice touch."

A Mona Lisa smile appeared on Lara's face as she focused on the flower. "I forgot about that. Perhaps you weren't being too dramatic, after all."

"Oh?" he asked innocently.

"I found that bud on my office doorstep this morning. No card or message was attached. Very mysterious."

"Just the rose, nothing else?"

"Yes, now that you mention it. There was something else. A dead shrub. Now I wonder what that could mean? It sounds rather sinister, doesn't it?"

Tanner laughed out loud. "That was a rosebush, and it's just dormant, not dead."

"Aha!" Lara cried, jabbing an accusing finger at his chest. "Obviously you were the one that left it there, or you wouldn't have known it was a rosebush, dead or dormant!"

"All right, you got me." Tanner raised his hands in surrender, then spoiled the humble look with a leer. "Now what are you going to do with me?"

"I'm not sure," Lara admitted. "Tell me what they meant and then I'll decide."

"That's no mystery. It's Valentine's Day. Men are supposed to give their women roses."

"Yes," she agreed, "but they usually give them live ones."

"That rosebush is alive. In fact, it's much more alive than a cut rose like this." Tanner gave the bloom in the vase a light flick with one blunt fingertip.

"Okay, men usually give women cut roses, then, if you insist on being technical."

Tanner clucked his tongue in disappointment. "Here I thought I was being so romantic, and it was all a waste."

"Not at all. I thought the single rose was beautiful, and that stick thing certainly added a dash of intrigue," Lara protested, anxious not to hurt his feelings.

"But you missed the point," Tanner complained.

"Oh? Maybe you should enlighten me then. Why the cut rose and the dead—I mean dormant—rosebush?"

Tanner removed the blooming rose from the vase, pausing for a moment to breathe in the musky fragrance before offering it to Lara. Hesitantly she reached out to accept it. Instead of letting go when she grasped the stem, however, he covered the hand now holding the rose with both of his.

"A single rose is like a night of passion," he explained in a slow, husky voice. "Beautiful while it lasts, but all too soon its time is gone and the beauty fades to just a memory."

Lara felt her heart fill her throat, her breath cut off by fear. Tanner tightened his hold on her hand, leaning close to see her expression revealed by the flickering light of the candles.

"But love is the root from which the passion springs," he continued. "As long as that root is nourished and cared for, the plant will thrive and passion will bloom again and again. Though it may seem barren through the winter, it will branch out again each spring. And though it may seem spent and wilted through the summer drought, the root that survives the heat will put forth its most beautiful blooms of all in the autumn."

He let go with one hand and raised it to gently cup her cheek with his palm, lifting her face for his kiss. Lara closed her eyes as his lips brushed softly over hers.

"You gave me both the bloom and the root," she whispered against his mouth.

He nodded, drawing back slightly so that he could see her eyes. "One for the passion we've already shared and that is now a memory to be treasured. The other as my promise to love you and to continue bringing passion to that love for the rest of our lives."

It was one of those rare moments when Lara found herself at a loss for words. She had gone to all this trouble to plan an evening of reality for Tanner and herself. But who could expect reality from a farmer who proved to also be a poet? Who needed it?

Unable to think of anything else, she simply kissed Tanner back. There were no protests or stalling tactics when he pushed the table away and lowered her to the rug. Then the poet farmer undid the tiny pearl buttons one by one and accepted that which Lara gave freely.

And true to her nature, Lara completely disregarded the wrappings on her present, shamelessly ripping his shirt apart in her eagerness to possess its contents.

6

THE LAST STREAK of pink had just stolen across the sky when Lara woke for the second time the next morning. It was tempting to stay in the warm cocoon created by her grandmother's quilts, but Tanner's absence greatly diminished the pleasure of sleeping late.

She had said as much to him when he had gotten out of bed just before dawn. His answer didn't surprise her anymore. She had heard it often enough in the last month and a half. If they quit seeing each other and just got married, all their problems would be solved.

It was a twisted kind of logic, though. Tempting, but twisted. Lara knew there were still far too many unanswered questions standing between them, the most important beginning with a capital *J*.

She threw back the heavy covers, steeling herself against the rush of cold air that greeted her bare skin. Forgoing her usual, eye-opening shower, she quickly slipped into cornflower-print long johns; jeans, a sweater and an old pair of hiking boots followed. In a brief moment of inspiration she retrieved the rosebush Tanner had given her yesterday, then dragged herself out of the house, still yawning.

Maybe Tanner's homestead would provide the answers he himself seemed reluctant to divulge. As she drove toward the McElroy farm, Lara tried to recall the details of the old farmhouse, thinking perhaps it would provide some clues about its occupant. Unfortunately, the one time she had been inside, she had been too preoccupied with its drunken owner to pay much attention to the house itself.

For some strange reason, she retained an impression of Latin American influence. But that was surely wrong. She must have confused Tanner's home with those in the Santa Fe style that had been so popular in Houston. Modern primitive hardly seemed appropriate for a bachelor farmer in the rural delta of Northeast Arkansas.

Oh, well, she would be able to see for herself soon enough. Lara turned onto the gravel strip that led up to the clapboard house. She didn't get out immediately, choosing to sit quietly for a moment while she scrutinized the outside.

The house itself was painted white, accented by a slate-gray roof with matching shutters. The color scheme was repeated in the large stones comprising the front porch, which stretched from one end of the house to the other.

Although the house was surrounded on all sides by fields, a small space had been reserved for a more traditional lawn, dotted with brown areas that would no doubt become flower beds and a vegetable patch in the spring. It appeared Tanner's hobby was gardening, which didn't really surprise her. Growing things was a way of life in Arkansas, whether the crop was families or flowers or food.

The barren, thorny bushes marching in a straight line on either side of the porch steps were obviously kin to the rosebush occupying the passenger seat beside her. If Tanner balked at letting her come inside, she figured she could use the bush as an excuse for visiting. Offering to plant it here at his home should reassure him that she was very serious about their relationship.

Coming here was definitely a better idea than the one she'd concocted for last night. She should have realized that the romantic dinner she'd planned wasn't going to get them anywhere but the bedroom. She had made a major tactical error there. Romance was not what they were missing. No, what they needed were details, the sort of stuff that allows a relationship to withstand the changing seasons of marriage.

Lara knew Tanner was intelligent, had an excellent sense of humor, possessed a definite romantic streak, and was undeniably attractive. There was no doubt as to their physical compatibility, as well. But there were still too many unanswered questions.

She had intended to quiz him on some multiple choice items last night. What kind of books did he like to read? Who were his favorite authors? Which TV shows did he refuse to miss? Where did he like to go on vacation? How often did he get away from the farm?

Then, of course, there were still the big questions. How did he feel about her career? When they had children, would he expect her to give up her practice? Would the amount of her income threaten his ego?

The realization of how little she and Tanner knew about each other rolled over Lara like a giant snowball. She had been sleeping with the man for six weeks and she didn't even know if he was a Democrat, a Republican or an independent.

They had found their common ground in the bedroom, exploring each other's bodies, instead of in the little bits and pieces of information that are usually discovered on those first few dates when two people are forced to make idle conversation.

Intimate discussion by candlelight as they sat on the rug where they had first made love obviously was not the answer. Lara groaned out loud as she realized just how stupid that idea had been. She had set up an evening designed for seduction, not soul-baring.

Lara had an uneasy feeling that Tanner was not going to take her fact-finding mission very well. She was sure it was not a coincidence that Tanner, who had to be shoved out of bed during the week when she was in a rush to leave, always left before the sun arrived on the weekends, those precious days when she could have lingered in bed with him.

If he was so sure about their being right for each other, why was he so reluctant for them to get to know each other better? With renewed determination Lara got out of the car and forged up the steps. The only way to get the answer to that question, as well as all the others, was to ask.

Tanner had just poured his second cup of coffee when the doorbell rang. He never got a chance to drink it. Lara took it out of his hand the second after he opened the door. She had chugged half of it down before he could even get out her name.

"Thanks," she said, pushing a stunned Tanner aside and walking in. "That's just what I needed. You know, I'm really not worth a damn in the mornings until I've had my coffee."

"Glad to be of service," Tanner said. "What's the matter? Was your coffee machine not working?"

"No. At least, I don't think so. I didn't try it. I just thought there was no point in making two pots when we can share one, right?"

"Right." The reflex answer came out with a strong trace of doubt. Hearing it, Tanner gave up trying to pretend he wasn't surprised to see her. "Lara, what are you doing here? I thought you would be sleeping in this morning. It is Saturday, you know."

"I know." She sighed, moving in to press her body against the long, hard length of his. "But it just wasn't the same, lying in bed without you."

Tanner felt his ego grow six inches. "Missed me, did you?"

"Mmm, just a tad. You don't mind me coming over, do you?"

He hesitated a telling second before answering. "No, of course not."

"In that case, do you think I could have a refill?" she asked, raising his now empty coffee cup between them.

"Sure," he said with a certain lack of conviction. "Help yourself."

She stood on tiptoe for a moment, planting a fleeting kiss on his lips. "Thanks, I will. You just go on about your business, I can make myself at home."

Lara moved into the foyer, glancing casually around. Straight ahead were the stairs leading up to the bedrooms. To her right was the living room, which, much to her amazement, conformed to the "modern primitive" impression she had thought must be a mistake.

Remembering the ruse she had used to get herself in, Lara quickly smothered the desire to examine the room more thoroughly, turning to the left toward the dining room and the kitchen that was located just beyond. She had discovered that room during her search for aspirin the night she had driven Tanner home from the Jube. She headed there now, taking his mug with her.

Tanner followed her, but stopped in the kitchen doorway, watching as she poured herself a refill and then pulled out a chair at the breakfast table, shamelessly commandeering the newspaper he had been reading just minutes before.

"Just how long were you planning on staying?" he asked, noting that she didn't seem to be in much of a hurry.

"Trying to get rid of me?"

"No, no," he said quickly. "I was just curious."

Each sip of coffee increased the sharpness with which Lara's mind was functioning. It was obvious to her that Tanner was trying to be nice about her surprise invasion, but he definitely was not comfortable with her being there.

Good, she thought. She was tired of being the only one who felt as if she had fallen down the rabbit hole. It wouldn't hurt to throw this usually self-assured man off balance for a while. Maybe that was the best way to discover some of the answers to her questions.

"I thought you usually caught up on your paperwork on Saturdays," he ventured.

"I do. Usually. I decided to give myself a day off, though. All work and so on."

"Yeah," Tanner said, "I know what you mean. Too bad farmers can't take a day off. But crops and weather refuse to be put on hold. I'm even more behind than usual, since I had to spend all day yesterday at the bank."

Lara ignored his hint, brushing it aside and grasping the information about the bank instead. "I forgot about that. What sort of meeting was it?"

He winced, wishing too late that he hadn't brought up that particular subject. "Oh, just the usual."

"I'm not sure I know what the usual is in the farming industry," Lara persisted.

Tanner thrust his hand through his hair, wondering how he could get out of this particular conversation with a little pride left still intact. He had a strong urge to just tell Lara it was none of her business, but that wasn't exactly true. If she married him, it would be very much her business and her problem.

"I'm trying to get financing for a new irrigation system. The old one is just about shot, and I'm afraid another summer like last year will do it in completely."

"Can't the old system be patched up?"

"It has been patched and repatched. No, I'm definitely going to have to have a new one." Tanner lifted his head to study the woman sitting across from him. She didn't seem particularly alarmed by his financial prospects. Nor did she seem to be oozing pity for him. Her attitude could be described best as simply matter-of-fact.

"Do you think the bank will come through with a loan?"

"Well, farmers aren't exactly their favorite customers at the moment."

Lara nodded sympathetically. "Don't you just hate banks? I mean, they're there to lend money, but they only want to lend it to people who don't need it. You wouldn't believe what a hard time they gave me about my business loan."

Tanner arched his eyebrows in surprise. "You took out a loan?"

"I had to. How else was I supposed to pay for my half of the rent, my secretary's salary, office expenses and a law library before I had even begun to practice? Oh, and let's not forget malpractice insurance."

"Malpractice? I thought that was something doctors worried about, not lawyers," Tanner said.

"It's become a big issue with lawyers, too. The latest litigation trend has been clients suing their lawyers when they don't win their cases." Lara shook her head in disgust. "I even know one attorney who specializes in legal malpractice cases. He was sued for malpractice himself after losing a case against another lawyer."

"You're kidding." Tanner laughed.

"Nope, it can become a never-ending circus. A client just keeps suing until he gets a verdict he likes."

"Well, I'm sure you won't have anything to worry about. Word around here is that you are an excellent attorney."

"Oh really?" Lara smiled. "Well, I'm glad to hear the Morristown communications network is right about some things." Her smile dissolved quickly. "Still, it only takes one screwup to ruin a practice."

"I can't imagine you making a mistake," Tanner said loyally.

"Thanks, but it's easy to do. A lawyer has to make a lot of decisions strictly on instinct." She thought of yesterday and her meeting with Susan.

Tanner watched the play of emotions across her face, recognizing the puzzled frown that meant Lara was second-guessing herself. "What is it? Is one of your cases giving you trouble right now?"

"Oh, I just gave some advice to a client yesterday, and now I'm not sure if it was right or not."

"Why don't you tell me about it?" Tanner offered. "Maybe an objective opinion would help."

She hesitated for a moment, torn between her personal need to discuss it with him and her professional responsibility to her client. Finally she settled on a compromise, giving him the gist of the situation without mentioning any specifics.

"One of my divorce cases is considering a reconciliation."

"Is that so bad?"

"Not necessarily. I'm just concerned that ... my client ... might be considering it for the wrong reasons."

"Such as?"

"They are having second thoughts about the effect the divorce will have on their children and about the economics of the situation."

"Is that so surprising?" Tanner asked.

"No, not really. People often do stay together for those very reasons. Sometimes it works out, sometimes it doesn't."

"But you don't think it's enough in this particular case?"

"I'm not sure." Lara caught her lower lip between her teeth as she considered Susan's case. "I happen to think a lot of this particular client, and I know that my client has been hurt a great deal. I'm not sure that the ... spouse deserves a second chance."

"So what kind of advice did you give your client?" Tanner asked.

"To just go slow. I suggested that the couple try dating again, as opposed to a full reconciliation. Take their time and use this as a chance to really get to know each other."

He didn't criticize her counsel out loud, but Lara knew from the way he lowered his gaze and tightened his mouth that Tanner didn't agree with her. "What would you have advised?" she asked defensively.

"Well, I don't think sitting on the fence will get them anywhere. If they really want to get back together, they should do it before things grow worse. But if things were bad enough to make them separate in the first place, I think your client should probably just dump the spouse and cut his or her losses."

"You make it sound like a bad investment."

"Isn't that what relationships are, investments of time?" Tanner asked.

She carefully considered the analogy for a moment before agreeing. "Okay, I'll buy that, but part of making a wise investment is researching all the possibilities before making a decision. All I suggested was that my client test the market before deciding either way."

Tanner nodded, "Not bad advice, I guess, as long as your client doesn't take too long to consider."

"You're damn right it was good advice," Lara said indignantly, gaining confidence after hearing her arguments expressed. "In fact, maybe it's just the kind I should be giving myself."

"What do you mean?" he asked.

"I mean that maybe we should start dating and give ourselves a chance to really get to know each other, before we start getting serious."

"We've been dating for six weeks," Tanner protested, "and I've been serious from day one."

"No," she corrected him. "We have been sleeping together for six weeks." When he would have interrupted her, she placed her hand over his mouth and shook her head. "And no, it isn't the same thing. We may know how to please each other in bed, but we don't know a damn thing about pleasing each other outside the bedroom. You didn't even tell me about the bank meeting, and it was obviously important to you."

"Is that what's giving you second thoughts?" Tanner asked. "You're afraid you'll be hitching yourself to a broken plough? Lara, I'm not going to pretend I'm ever going to get rich farming, but you admitted you aren't going to get rich practicing law here, either."

"I'm not talking about getting rich, Tanner. I am not talking about money at all. I am just saying that we need to know more about each other than we can learn by sleeping together."

Tanner shook his head angrily, visibly denying the truth in her words. "We know all we need to know. We're both here to stay. We have both planted our roots here, and we are going to do whatever it takes to keep them growing. That is what's important."

"Tanner, be reasonable," Lara pleaded. "Simply choosing to live in the same town isn't enough to base a relationship on."

"Well it's more than I had in common with Jodi!" he yelled back. The words echoed repeatedly in the silence that followed his outburst. Tanner pushed himself away from the table, turning his back to Lara as he stood, bracing himself against the kitchen counter.

"Damn, that isn't what I meant to say," he muttered quietly, almost to himself. "Jodi doesn't have anything to do with this."

"Doesn't she?" asked Lara. "Isn't she the reason you've never asked me over here? The reason you really didn't want to let me inside this morning?"

"No!" he denied sharply. "She has nothing to do with us."

"This is the house you shared with her, even if it was just for a few months out of the year. This is where you ate with her and talked with her and slept with her. And you don't want me here. Isn't that the truth, Tanner?"

"No," he repeated. "She doesn't have anything to do with us. As far as I'm concerned, she doesn't exist anymore."

"Oh, really, you're just going to wipe out seven years of your life just like that," she said, snapping her fingers.

"Why not? They didn't mean anything. I don't have anything to show for them." Tanner spun around to pin Laura with anguished eyes. "All that time was wasted just playing a stupid game with a woman who refused to grow up. I'm not playing games anymore, Lara."

"I'm not interested in games, either." Lara walked toward him, coming to a stop when she stood barely a foot away. "And I am also not interested in making the same old mistakes. I don't intend to become the strike-out queen when it comes to marriage. The next time I walk down the aisle will be the last. That is why I want to make sure I'm right."

"And what will it take to convince you?"

"I'm not sure," she admitted, "but it will take more than I've seen so far. We might as well start here, though." Lara was looking around the kitchen as she spoke, and he knew she was hinting at a tour of the house.

"You've been here before," he protested.

"Just that night I drove you home. I didn't realize then that I might be living here one day. That does rather change a woman's perspective, you know?"

Tanner hesitated, mentally reviewing the state of the house and its contents, trying to remember how much of Jodi's presence remained.

"You would expect me to live here if we ever did get married, wouldn't you, Tanner? If so, I think I'm entitled to the grand tour," Lara told him, pressing on.

He couldn't argue with her logic, Tanner decided, but he could stall. "Well, maybe. But there wouldn't be any problem with staying in your house, either."

"Wouldn't that be a little inconvenient for you?" Lara asked. "Besides, it is still my parents' house. I'm just renting it from them."

"Yeah, well, I guess we could decide that when the time comes. If you really want to see the place, why don't we start with the fields? I need to go out and check them, anyway. You might as well come along."

It wasn't exactly a gracious invitation, but Lara decided not to push her luck. She followed Tanner outside, scrambling onto the ATV behind him, wrapping her arms around his waist for security as they bounced along the dirt road that divided the fields.

Tanner stopped frequently to check the winter wheat crop that was now standing a few inches above the ground. Lara glanced up at the gray sky above them, remembering the forecast she had heard on the radio on her way over. "They say it might snow tomorrow. Will it hurt the crop?"

He shook his head. "Not at this stage. If we get one of those Easter blizzards, it'll be a problem, but those are pretty rare. Right now, the more snow the better. It'll help boost the water table."

Lara nodded, absorbing the information along with the other bits of data she was gleaning from him as they continued. He had just finished showing her the irrigation lines he intended to replace, when they heard a loud honk blaring across the quiet landscape.

"Must be Hank," Tanner said. "I forgot he was coming by today."

"Not Hank Metcalf?" Lara asked weakly, knowing the answer even before Tanner confirmed her guess.

"Yeah, he's supposed to deliver my fuel today. I better go help him tank up."

He was already swinging his leg back over the ATV's seat as he spoke, so Lara knew he'd missed the grimace that crossed her face.

"Coming?" he prompted, when she made no move to join him. She was tempted to just say she would wait here in the middle of the deserted field, but knew he would not understand. With a strong sense of trepidation, she resumed her seat behind him, silently praying that Hank had taken her advice as well as Susan had.

HANK METCALF was a burly man, about an inch short of six feet. What he lacked in height, though, he more than made up for in bulk. A stranger could be forgiven for thinking that a significant percentage of his mass was fat, but Lara knew better. She remembered Hank's days on the high school football team. Hank the Tank was one hundred percent pure beef.

From Hank's expression when he realized who was riding behind Tanner, Lara knew that this time he was going to be one mean bull. She wasn't proud of herself for using Tanner as a shield, but having his large frame between Hank and herself was definitely reassuring. Any minute now she expected the former linebacker to paw the ground and charge.

Susan's estranged husband completely ignored Tanner's greeting, brushing the farmer's hand aside to shake a large, meaty fist at Lara.

"I've been looking for you, Jamison. Just what the hell do you think you're doing, trying to come between me and my wife?" Hank's face was red with rage, his massive body trembling with fury.

"I'm not trying to do anything but my job, Hank."

"You're trying to split us up," he insisted. "You couldn't hold on to your marriage, so you're trying to screw up everyone else's."

"You seem to be doing quite well at screwing up your marriage all by yourself." Lara was trying to stay calm, but it was becoming increasingly difficult. She didn't like being afraid of someone, so she chose instead to be angry. "It has nothing to do with my personal life. Susan hired me as her attorney. I simply gave the best legal advice I had to my client."

"And that just happens to be the kind that will allow you to keep sucking legal fees out of people who can barely afford to make their house payments," Hank accused.

"Both of you calm down. Now!" Tanner interjected before Lara could make a comeback.

Hank didn't even spare the farmer a glance. "This isn't your problem, Tanner. Just stay out of it."

Tanner laughed. "You talk to my woman that way and start shaking your fist at her, and you want me to stay out of it? No way. If you want to get to her, you're going to have to go through me, Hank."

The look the bull tossed to Tanner then clearly indicated that wouldn't be a problem, as far as he was concerned. Fear for Tanner's safety cut through Lara's outrage. She slipped under his arm to confront Hank without the shield of Tanner's body between them. *No sense in both of them getting killed*, she thought ruefully.

"I can't say I am sorry about the advice I gave her, Hank. Your actions right now don't exactly commend you as a family man," Lara pointed out.

"That's because, thanks to you, I don't have a family anymore."

"If you lost your family, it's your doing, not mine. You should have thought of that before you betrayed Susan's trust."

"That's none of your business," Hank told her.

Lara shook her head. "You're wrong. It became my business when Susan hired me to represent her. Frankly, I'm surprised she even considered giving you a second chance. The way you're acting now, though, I doubt that will last long."

Hank jumped at her, but found Tanner's large hand planted against his chest. "Everything would have been okay, if you had just agreed to drop the proceedings. You're the one that ruined my second chance," he protested.

"If your attempts at reconciliation have been ruined, it's your fault, not mine," Lara corrected him.

Tanner placed both of his hands on Hank's shoulders, using his height advantage to push the other man back. "Calm down, Hank. All Lara did was ask Susan to take things slow. She's sitting on the fence right now. At least she was, if you haven't scared her back over to the other side."

A dark red flush crept up Hank's neck. "I have a right to be angry. She was going to let me come back until Lara interfered."

"Lara was just doing her job," Tanner insisted. "Any lawyer would have given Susan the same advice, if they hadn't talked her into skipping a reconciliation altogether. Lara did you a favor, pal. Whether you realize it or not."

Hank dragged his eyes away from his target and stared back at Tanner incredulously. "Convincing my wife not to take me back is doing me a favor? Please! Don't let her do me any more."

"Susan was going to take you back, all right, but just for the kids' sake." Tanner ignored the gasp he heard from Lara. Hell, Hank had a right to know what his wife was thinking. *Confidentiality be damned.* "What kind of marriage would you have had under those circumstances? Your kids are going to be out of the house in just a few more years. What's going to hold you two together then?"

"I could have made her love me again by then. I still love her. That would have held us together." Hank's voice broke, and it was clear he was trying to convince himself as much as Tanner and Lara.

"Maybe, maybe not," Tanner hedged. "But this way you have a chance to make her fall in love with you all over again. Now you won't have to spend the next few years wondering if she's going to leave you when the kids go."

Hank shook his head, brushing away the tears that threatened to spill down his broad, tanned cheeks. "No. I've lost any chance I had at getting her back."

"Not if you start acting like the man she fell in love with the first time."

Both men turned in surprise to stare at Lara.

"I'll admit I'm not your biggest fan right now, Hank. Any man who cheats on a woman like Susan is a fool. I suppose you must have some good points, or she would never have married you in the first place. Maybe if you can uncover those, she'll still take you back." Lara stepped closer, staring directly at the man who had hurt one of her best friends. "It is all up to you, though. I've got nothing to do with it at this stage."

"You've got nothing to lose but Susan, pal," Tanner added. "Give it all you've got."

Hank swallowed hard, then nodded sharply. He raised his hand again and shook one thick finger at Lara. "And I'll show both you and Susan why she'd be a fool not to take me back. You'll see."

"You do that, Hank," Lara said. "All I want is to see Susan happy."

Tanner pounded the burly man on the back, breaking the tension surrounding them. "Come on, Hank. Let's get this fuel unloaded. How about fixing some more coffee, Lara?"

She nodded and headed toward the kitchen, accepting the wifely chore with a meekness completely out of character for her. She would have used any pretense in order to get away from both men. One had challenged her professional integrity, and the other had violated her personal trust.

Angrily she searched for the coffee can, opening cupboards where she knew it couldn't possibly be, just for the satisfaction of slamming the doors shut again. She knew it was a childish reaction, but it was either slam and bang or scream. At that moment she didn't care about her mother's lectures on mature behavior or her admonitions about leaving closed doors shut when visiting someone else's home.

By the time the men were finished with their work, Lara had their coffee ready and had brewed up with it a whole new head of steam. She poured a cup for herself and joined them at the table, sitting quietly as Tanner kept the conversation firmly on farm topics. She didn't miss the glances that Hank aimed at her, nor did she underestimate the determination she saw in his bottomless, black eyes. Right now, though, Hank Metcalf was the least of her worries.

When they finally walked him to the door, she accepted the handshake Hank offered, taking note of his strength as she felt him grasp her much smaller palm.

"After I move back in, Susan and I'll have you two over for dinner," he said, clearly challenging her to deny his statement.

Lara said nothing, her poker face firmly in place as she reclaimed her hand.

"We'll look forward to it," Tanner answered for her, wrapping his arm around Lara's shoulders.

As Hank pulled away, Tanner moved to stand behind her, gently massaging her shoulders, apparently attempting to ease the tension that kept her standing ramrod-straight. Lara deliberately stepped away from the comforting touch. She really wasn't in the mood to be comforted at the moment. Not by him.

7

"REMEMBER OUR DISCUSSION about malpractice earlier?" she asked.

Tanner shifted his weight uncomfortably. "It wasn't a breach of confidence," he insisted. "You never told me your client's name. It's not your fault I guessed Susan was the one you were talking about."

"I doubt the ethics committee will see it that way," Lara said.

"Don't be silly," Tanner protested, "Susan isn't going to file a complaint. The ethics committee will never know."

"I will know, and it doesn't make me feel very good about myself. I take my professional responsibility very seriously, Tanner. I don't like making mistakes."

"Well, damn it, a husband has a right to know what his wife is thinking."

"Only if she chooses to tell him," Lara argued. "Susan trusted me, and I have betrayed that trust."

"No, you didn't, I did and I apologize. But can you blame me for wanting to help them get back together? Hank really loves Susan."

"Then why did he cheat on her?" Lara asked.

"Oh, come on, it's not like it was an all-out affair. It was a onetime thing. A one-night stand."

"Sure," Lara grunted. "That's what they all say."

"Well, in Hank's case, I believe it's true."

"And that's supposed to make it okay?"

"No, of course not. I never said that. But maybe it does make it more forgivable. Hank made a mistake. People do, you know."

"So you think Susan should take him back?"

"Yes, I do."

"You realize that you just did a one-eighty. A while ago, when my client was anonymous, you thought she should dump the guy. You said she should cut her losses."

"I didn't know all the circumstances then," Tanner said. "Susan and Hank have been together too long and have too much going for them to throw it all away."

"What about you and Jodi?"

Where the hell did that come from? he wondered. Lara might as well have dropped a bomb on him. He wouldn't have been any more surprised.

"There is no me and Jodi," he reminded her quietly.

"Not now, maybe. But there was, and if she came back, there might be again."

"Jodi won't be back." He spoke with such certainty, she almost believed him.

"Look," Tanner said, jumping in before Lara could push the topic further. "I'm sorry about violating your trust with Susan. It won't happen next time, okay?"

"You're damn right," Lara agreed, "because there's not going to be a next time."

Tanner lunged forward, swiftly grasping Lara's arms before she could turn away from him. "Now wait a second. You're not going to use this as an excuse to drive a wedge between us. I won't let you."

"I'm not trying to do any such thing," she assured him. When he had relaxed his grip slightly, she continued. "I just won't discuss my work with you again, ever."

"Lara!" Tanner started to argue with her, then changed his mind. Number one, he didn't have a good defense at that moment, and number two, he wasn't sure how to deal with an infuriated Lara. There was no doubt that she was furious with him. He would reestablish himself as a confidant some other time. Right now he just wanted to make up and get back into her good graces.

"Look, it's been a long day. We're both tired and stressed out." He paused for a moment, then added on a note of inspiration, "And hungry. Why don't we stop at a fast-food place on the way back to your house?"

"Why go to my house at all?" Lara parried. "I fixed dinner last night. That means it is your turn tonight. I'll just watch TV while you get something ready."

She was settled in the big, leather easy chair in the living room before he could think of a logical reason why they shouldn't stay. But that didn't stop him from trying.

"Lara, I'm a lousy cook. I'll buy us a pizza instead. And since the pizza place is much closer to your house, it makes a lot more sense to go there."

"I'm really not in the mood for pizza," Lara said, dashing his hopes for an easy victory. "Whatever you whip up will be just fine. I'm not a picky eater."

"But I really don't have anything to fix," Tanner protested.

"How about two of those steaks you have in the freezer? You also have several bakers in the potato bin, and I'm sure I saw some salad fixings in the refrigerator." She smiled at his defeated expression. "I just happened to notice them while I was fixing the coffee."

"You were looking for coffee in the freezer?"

"You never know. People sometimes store things in the oddest places. For example, I found this in with the potatoes." Lara stood again in order to pull a crumpled postcard from some Mexican hole-in-the-wall out of her back pocket.

Tanner recognized it instantly. "I must have missed the trash can," he growled, snatching the piece of mail out of her hand. "Maybe we should discuss the matter of confidentiality a little more, after all."

"Fine," she agreed. "I suggest a pact. I'll trust you enough to discuss my work, when you trust me enough to discuss your life."

"Jodi isn't my life, she's just part of my past. A very insignificant part," he added with emphasis.

"Right," Lara scoffed, "an insignificant part that just lasted seven years, and who's coming back to make it eight."

Tanner's jaw clenched angrily. "You read it?"

"Well, of course, I read it," she said. "It's a postcard. Everybody reads postcards. Most people don't write confidential messages on the back of something that's exposed to every wandering eye."

"You had no right," Tanner argued.

"And you had no right to let me believe everything is over between the two of you, when it isn't."

"It is, as far as I'm concerned."

"Really? It doesn't sound like it."

"How am I supposed to prove it, Lara? I don't have a divorce decree. Jodi and I were never married. There were no bonds between us. There was no commitment. How can I prove it's over, when there wasn't anything to start with?" Tanner demanded.

"If there wasn't anything to start with, then why did you wait for her for seven years?"

"Because I was a fool," Tanner admitted. "I fooled myself into believing that there was something where there wasn't. I'm not particularly proud of the fact, so you'll have to excuse me if I don't advertise it."

"But Jodi says she's coming back!"

"Not to stay! She has always said she'd be back, but she never stays. It doesn't mean anything."

"But what if this time she did want to stay?" Lara persisted. "You just said that Susan and Hank have been together too long to just throw it all away. Why doesn't the same thing apply to you and Jodi?"

"For crying out loud, Lara, you sound like you want me to take her back. Are you really ready to throw away what *we* have?"

"I'd rather do it now than later," she said. "Lord, Tanner. What if I had said yes the first time you asked me to marry you, and then Jodi came back? What would you have done then?"

"I would have said 'Hello, Jodi. I would like you to meet my wife Lara.' What do you think I would have done?"

"I'm serious, Tanner," she said, and the expression on her face could not have been more serious.

"So am I," he said. "I'm not waiting around the rest of my life to find out what Jodi means each time she says she'll be back. As far as I'm concerned, she no longer exists."

"Really?" Lara asked. "Then why don't you want me in this house? Isn't it because she's still here? I haven't tried to be nosy, Tanner. But I have eyes. I can see. If she doesn't exist, why is it that I can see her in every corner of this room?"

Lara swept the living room with her gaze, taking in the photographs scattered everywhere, the wall hangings from South America, the Indian pottery that lay on the shelves—all the little touches that she knew instinctively had come from Jodi.

"You know what's funny? I came over here today, because I thought maybe this house would tell me more about you, tell me the things that you won't. But the only person this house tells me about is Jodi. Look at this place, Tanner. You have created a damn shrine for her."

He sank wearily into the brown leather couch, burying his head in his hands ostrich style, as if he hoped that everything of Jodi's would just disappear. When he spoke again, it was in a voice so quiet and lifeless that Lara almost didn't recognize it as being his.

"I didn't create anything for her," he said. "These are just things she left here over the years."

"Over the years? Most of this furniture looks new."

"The furniture is mine," he admitted with reluctance.

"Obviously bought with her in mind," Lara noted.

"No, it's just . . . I don't know. It is just the stuff that attracted me."

"Really?" Lara glanced casually at the modern, leather sofa and chairs, accented by touches of Latin America. To be honest, the room was gorgeous, but it didn't match the man she thought she was coming to know. It certainly didn't match the antiques she had found in the other rooms or the old-fashioned gardens outside.

"Forgive me, Tanner," she continued, "but didn't it attract you because you were trying to make a home for Jodi, the kind of home you thought might convince her to stay put?"

"I don't know! I didn't think it was necessary to psychoanalyze my choice of couch." Suddenly restless, he began to prowl around, a caged lion tormented relentlessly by a tamer with a chair. "Look, if you don't like this stuff, it's no problem. We will just throw it out, okay?"

"But that's what I don't understand, Tanner. Why haven't you thrown it out? If you're so determined to pretend that Jodi never existed, so determined to wipe her out of your life, why didn't you start here? In this house?"

"I don't know. It just didn't seem that important. Maybe men just aren't bothered by things like that."

"I'm sorry," Lara said, "but I don't buy that. You noticed it enough to buy it in the first place. I would have thought that would have made it even less desirable to have around when it didn't work."

"Don't worry, I'll get rid of it immediately, just so we don't have to have this same ridiculous argument again."

"It's not ridiculous!"

"Isn't it? Isn't this just some little psychological game you lawyers play when you don't have any valid arguments left?" Tanner demanded, turning on her suddenly, shifting the question of motivation to his antagonist. With the smooth grace of a predatory animal he rose from the couch and began to bear down upon her.

"Just what does that mean?" Lara demanded, her instinctive retreat betraying the bravado in her voice.

"It means that I'm not going to let you distract me from the real issue," Tanner said as he ruthlessly closed in. "I'm not the one who is stalling here." He slowly backed her into a corner.

"I'm not the one who's trying to deny our relationship." He planted a fist on the wall to her left. "I'm not the one who's hung up on previous lovers." He nailed the wall on her right.

"You are the only one trying to squirm out of making a commitment," he finished. "Not me."

Lara pressed her hands against his chest, trying to hold on to the very small amount of space he had left her. "I'm not trying to squirm out of anything. I just refuse to be trapped in an impossible situation."

"The only impossible thing here are your demands. What is it you really want, Lara? Or don't you know?" He didn't give her a chance to answer, pushing on relentlessly. "It sounded like you and your first husband had plenty in common. All those little things you seemed to be so concerned about. But what good did it do? You still walked out on him."

"I didn't walk out on him," Lara protested. "We got a divorce because we had irreconcilable differences."

"There's a nice catchphrase," Tanner sneered. "Another one of those fancy lawyerisms designed to cover every circumstance." The sarcasm dripped heavily off his tongue, leaving a bitter taste in his mouth.

"It happens to fit the circumstances," she said.

"Sure," he drawled. "You wanted a family and he didn't. An irreconcilable difference. So how come you go into a deep freeze whenever I suggest getting you pregnant?"

"Maybe because I'm not so sure I want you to be the father of my children."

Tanner flexed his elbows, pressing closer, forcing her back against the wall. "Why not? I'm offering you everything you claim you want out of a marriage, but you're still not buying. Why not, Lara?"

"I didn't realize the offer was good for a limited time only. Maybe you should have been a little more specific in your terms," she responded, thrusting out her chin in a way that should have warned Tanner she had been pushed as far as she would allow.

"Maybe you should make up your mind about what it is you really want," he retaliated, ignoring the warning sign. "I don't think Jodi is really what's bothering you at all. You're just using her as a way out."

"That's ridiculous."

"Is it?" he asked. "Isn't the real truth that you're just like her? You are incapable of making a commitment, because you keep thinking there might be something better around the bend." He spat angry words into Lara's face, and she didn't like it one little bit.

"I forgave you the last time you confused me with Jodi, but not this time." She ignored Tanner's blank look; if he couldn't remember their first meeting, it was his own damned fault.

"You thought I was Jodi that night at the Jube, and I blamed it on the liquor. But there aren't any excuses this time," she said, her defenses gathering strength as her sense of righteous indignation grew.

"I refuse to let you punish me for another woman's mistakes. Maybe Jodi had her own reasons for not making a commitment to you. That's between you and her. It's got nothing to do with me."

"Then why do you keep bringing her up?" Tanner pounded once on the wall for each of the last four words, his frustration eating away at what was left of his control.

"I don't."

Tanner grunted harshly.

"All right, maybe I do, but just so I can find out what feelings you still have for her. I need to know if you are ready to love someone else. To love me."

"My God," he swore, "can't you tell? Doesn't the way we make love answer that? No woman has ever made me feel a tenth of what you do. Doesn't that tell you something?"

Tanner lowered his hands to clench her shoulders, dragging her up against his chest. "Remember that first night we were together? You said it was destiny, that we were meant to be together. How can you deny that now?"

"I'm not trying to." Lara threw her head back in anguish. "Maybe we were destined to be lovers, but that doesn't mean it should go any further. Being good in bed isn't enough to make a relationship work.

"I don't have any magical answers, Tanner. Maybe I'll wake up tomorrow and I'll know that the past is over and we can finally go on together. Right now, all I can see is Jodi on the horizon, coming back to you, and I'm afraid you'll want her."

"Never!" he shouted. "That will never happen."

"Do you know how many times a day I hear someone say never? Susan Metcalf sat in my office and swore she would never take Hank back. Five months later I'm the only thing that stands between their reconciling."

When Tanner began to shake his head, repeating, "No, no, no," over and over, she cradled his face in her hands and forced him to listen.

"I hear it every day. Hell, I've said it myself. Never doesn't last very long, Tanner."

She slid a thumb over his mouth, keeping him silent. "A few weeks sleeping alone, a couple of holidays with no one to celebrate with, then that awful person we swear we hated doesn't seem so bad."

He grasped her hands, pulling them down, holding them clasped in his between their pounding hearts. "I've spent years sleeping alone. I've spent hundreds of holidays not celebrating at all, because Jodi wasn't here with me. And you're right, it did make me see her differently. It's what finally made me realize that I didn't want to love her anymore."

"That you didn't want to? Do you think it's that easy?" she asked. "You just decide you don't want to love her anymore, and all those feelings just go away? Is that what you think, Tanner?"

"Yes," he said. "I chose not to love her anymore."

"Loving isn't a choice, Tanner. It isn't something we choose to feel or not feel."

"Isn't it? Didn't you choose not to love your ex-husband?" Tanner insisted. "Didn't you choose to walk out on your marriage, because he couldn't or wouldn't give you what you wanted?"

"I chose not to live with him. I chose not to stay married to him. Those were my choices. I already told you that I still love him and probably always will, at least a little."

"Then you're a fool," Tanner said. "A fool to waste your emotions on someone who doesn't want them or deserve them. I'm not a fool. I can and will choose whom I love."

"Then what happens when you choose to stop loving me? If you can decide to stop loving Jodi just like that—" she snapped her fingers "—then what happens if you decide to stop loving me?"

"That's not going to happen!"

"I wish I could believe that, Tanner," she whispered. "I really wish I could, but I can't."

"I swear," he said, "I swear that I'll never stop loving you."

"And didn't you ever swear the same thing to Jodi?"

Tanner's silence answered for him. He searched for some way of denying it, some way to prove that those vows hadn't counted. When he couldn't find one, he tried to throw the problem back at her. "What about your vows to Kevin? Didn't you make the same promises to him?"

"Yes," she admitted freely, "and I'm not very proud of having broken them. That's why I'm determined not to make the same mistake again. I won't remarry unless I'm sure beyond a shadow of a doubt that it will be forever."

"Then what can I do to convince you?" Tanner asked. "You want me to throw everything out? You want me to burn the house down? I'll do it. Just tell me what it takes. You want me to hunt Jodi down and destroy her, so you will never have to worry about her coming back and luring me away? What do you want from me?"

"Time. I'm just asking for time."

"How much, then? Just tell me how much."

"I can't! Maybe someday..."

"Someday?" Tanner demanded. "I can tell you about someday, Lara. You say never doesn't last long. Well, I can tell you someday lasts an eternity. Jodi has been telling me someday for seven years, and now I'm hearing it from you."

Tanner dropped his hands, striding away with barely leashed violence. "It's no wonder I've gotten the two of you confused. What is it with women these days? I thought women were the ones who pushed for promises and commitments. What's wrong with you and Jodi?"

"Who says it has to be our problem?" Lara wanted to know. "You don't want to talk about your future or your past, but you don't hesitate to put all the blame on me and Jodi. Maybe you should take a long, hard look at yourself, Tanner. Maybe you are part of the problem."

"What could I have done to make two women so afraid of marriage?" Tanner asked.

"You've pushed too hard, for starters," Lara said. "I don't know about Jodi, but when somebody pushes me, I push back. Just because I'm not going down the same path or moving at the same speed you are, doesn't make me wrong, Tanner. Maybe you should quit yelling directions for a while and just follow. Quietly."

"Why should I follow someone who's walking in circles?" Tanner retorted. "At least I know where I'm headed."

"Maybe," Lara agreed, "but when it's the altar you're aiming for, it doesn't do you any good to arrive alone."

"Then come with me!" he pleaded.

"When I'm ready," she answered, "and not a moment sooner."

He couldn't take it anymore. Women were beyond him. Tanner had never felt more weary, more confused or more frustrated. "Damn it. Just get out, then," he ordered. "To hell with you. If you won't come with me, I'll find somebody else who will."

"That's your prerogative," Lara said, still refusing to surrender. Without another word she turned and marched through the door, head held high, her back stiff with pride.

SHE KNEW the facts of life were such that Tanner could find someone else far more easily than she could. But she also knew the odds were that anyone he married now would find herself in a lawyer's office down the road. Whether he admitted it or not, Tanner was too emotionally unstable to settle down with anyone at this time.

All the way home she told herself how right she was and how sorry he would be when he realized it. He would probably marry some desperate, man-hungry floozy and get her pregnant right away. Then Jodi would come back, and he'd be stuck with a woman he didn't love, a child that deserved better circumstances, and a mountain of legal bills when his wife realized what a fool she had been. Jodi would be furious that he hadn't waited for her and would disappear forever.

It would serve him right, too. Maybe Tanner would even ask Lara to represent him. On the other hand, maybe she would represent his wife. That would show him.

Then, when he came crawling back, admitting how right Lara had been and how wrong he was, maybe then she would think about seeing him again. If she was still available. And she might not be.

Yes, that would be even better. Maybe she would have another husband by then and a baby. *Make that twins.* That would show him. Every time he saw her children he would be forced to remember that he might have been their father. If he had just been patient. If he had not been such a blasted idiot.

The plot for revenge continued to grow, right up to the moment she parked her car and unlocked her house. Lara stepped inside, closed the door and then sank to the floor, crying so hard she didn't even have the strength to run upstairs and fling herself onto the bed.

It was so unfair. So damnably unfair. What good was there in being right, when she still had to sleep alone? She wanted to feel him lying next to her. She wanted to sleep wrapped in his arms. Damn it, she wanted his baby. What good was there in being right, when it didn't give her any of the things she wanted?

TANNER KICKED the door shut behind Lara. It felt so good, he kicked it again, harder. Then he began to pound it with his fists until his hands were bruised. It still wasn't enough.

He grabbed a hand-painted, clay pot Jodi had sent him from Guatemala and threw it across the room, where it crashed against the stone fireplace. Better. Much better. He snatched a vase she had sent from Brazil and smashed it in the empty hearth. A statue from Venezuela followed it and was joined by a bowl

from Chile. Once unleashed, the violent emotions refused to stay pent-up any longer.

When he had broken every breakable piece that Jodi
had brought into his house, he began to gather the straw
baskets and woven blankets, piling them up outside
where he usually burned the trash, running back into
the house for more, returning each time with an arm-
load of painful memories.

He tore through the house, grabbing photos and
postcards to toss onto the pyre he was building. He
stripped the sheets from his bed and pulled more out of
the linen chest. All the sheets that they had slept on together. The closet was flung open and articles of clothing ripped from their hangers. Things Jodi had left
behind, things of his that she had borrowed.

Tanner didn't stop until he had removed every trace
of her from the house, even the leather chair and sofa.
Lara had been right. He had bought them for Jodi,
trying to bring the world she longed for into the house
he loved.

Now he would rid himself of her once and for all. He
poured gasoline onto the pile, struck a match and then
threw the flame onto the mass before he could change
his mind. He stood straight and tall, letting the blaze
consume all he had left of the seven-year love that had
plagued him.

The flames were so hot and he stood so close that
sweat poured from his body. His eyes filled with tears,
and he blamed them on the smoke that clogged the air.
Still he did not back away.

The fire fed itself greedily, steadily, roaring with satisfaction when it discovered a new morsel to satisfy its
hunger. It ate the photos and the postcards and still it

burned. It ravaged the leather couch and chair and still it burned. It engulfed the rugs and wall hangings, the clothes and the bed linens and still it burned.

Tanner began to believe that the fire would never be satisfied; it was waiting for something. But what more could he add? There was nothing left for Jodi, nothing but what was left in his heart, and that was not his to surrender.

Lara was right. He couldn't choose to give it up. It was not his choice. Love had a life of its own. The fire seemed to sigh heavily, giving up at last, leaving behind only a pile of ashes and an exhausted host.

It was over. The bitterness and the hatred were gone. The love was still there, but it was different, recast in a new mold by the heat of the fire, taking on a new existence. Tanner stamped out the dying embers, making sure that there were no sparks left that might leap out later to engulf what was left of his home.

The moon was already rising when he finally reentered his house. The living room appeared stark and naked to him. Nothing remained but shards of pottery and glass littering the fireplace.

Moving in the trancelike state of someone who had endured an incredible loss, Tanner swept up the pieces and threw them away. Then he went through the house, shutting the drawers he had emptied, closing the cupboards he had ransacked. As the night began to fade away, he finally lay down on a bare mattress, slipping quickly into a deep, dreamless sleep.

8

THE PUNGENT SMELL of smoke filled Tanner's nostrils. A coating of soot and ashes covered his body, irritating his skin. His eyes felt raw and swollen from the combined effects of smoke and tears. In the distance he could hear church bells ringing as the Sunday morning services ended.

Tanner's first waking thought was that he really should start going to church more often. Maybe a few sermons would tame the heathen impulses that had raged inside him last night. He must have been possessed; it was the only explanation for his almost satanic behavior.

Fighting the lethargy that threatened to keep him flat on his back, he shoved his feet into a pair of boots and went outside to view the desecration, hoping faintly that it had all been some horrible dream, the kind you woke up from almost believing it had really happened.

But it had happened. The filthy clothes he still wore and a glance at the naked living room on his way out confirmed that the nightmare had been reality. Outside he found the remains of the bonfire.

Tanner shuffled through the ashes, occasionally reaching down to retrieve a piece of metal that hadn't disintegrated in the flames. He felt numb and confused, as if he were attending the funeral of a loved one who had died an unexpected and tragic death.

Perhaps it *was* a funeral of sorts. A cremation of Jodi and what they had once had. It was easier to think of it that way. Easier to accept it as something civilized like a burial service rather than a pagan sacrifice.

He paced around the site uncomfortably, trying to come to terms with himself. It was done. It was over. However much he might regret the way he had removed Jodi from his life, it was done now.

This was what it had been like when his father died, Tanner recalled. The pacing back and forth restlessly, feeling useless, because there was nothing that could be done anymore. It had taken a while for the pain and sadness to seep through the initial shock.

Was that how this would be?

First the numbness, then the pain, then the slow healing, until finally he felt whole again. Then there would just be occasional flashes. A laugh that sounded like hers. A joke that perhaps only she would have understood.

Maybe Lara was right. Maybe it would be a long time before he was ready for someone else in his life. It certainly wasn't fair to expect Lara to accept some man still half-crazed with the effects of grief. It had seemed to take forever before he had gotten to the pleasant-memories stage with his father. Would it take just as long to finally recover from loving Jodi?

Then he remembered the anger. How could he have forgotten the anger? When his father had died of lung cancer, after years of promising to quit smoking tomorrow, Tanner had been furious.

He had been angry with his father for continuing a habit known to be deadly. He had been angry with manufacturers who continued to sell something so harmful simply for profit. He had been angry with the government for not stopping it and the doctors for not curing it. He had never known he could hate so much.

How could he have forgotten the anger? That was what he had felt for the past few months. Anger. Fury. Outrage. Just another phase of grief.

He sifted a handful of ashes through his fingers. He didn't feel angry anymore. The fire had taken care of that. It had cleansed the debilitating hate, just as burning the fields cleared the stubble left after the harvest.

It had taken years to get past the denial stage, to accept the fact that he and Jodi weren't meant for each other. At least he had been able to breach the anger stage in a matter of months. Last night he had sunk into a rock-bottom depression, but he didn't have to let himself stay there.

Physical labor. That was what he needed. A little dirt and a lot of good, honest sweat. He grabbed a shovel from the tractor shed and began to scoop up the ashes, carrying them around the back of the house, where Grandmother McElroy's prize rose garden had once stood.

He hadn't kept up this garden as he had the ones in front. The roses that had survived here were scraggly and twisted. The arbor they surrounded leaned shakily, the paint peeling from its wooden frame. The hammock, which had once been large enough and strong enough to hold a pair of lovers, was now just a few rotten strands of rope, hanging from two rusty metal chains.

With no specific plan in mind and a fierce need to work, Tanner began digging up the roses that still showed promise of life, disposing of the ones that were nothing but dry rot. Then he tilled the ground and worked in the ashes from the fire, replanting the living bushes in the enriched soil.

Next he tested each beam that made up the arbor, replacing the ones that were weak or cracked. Then he scrounged in the shed for what was left of the white paint he had used on the house last year.

Hours later, the garden had been restored. Tanner stood back, covered with dirt and drenched with sweat, despite the cold air. It didn't look like much now. A few sticks, surrounding a simple, white structure. But Tanner was seeing as only a farmer could.

He saw limbs shooting out from the pruned branches, stretching upward, climbing the arbor to reach the sun. Tiny leaves uncurling to catch the dew. Buds forming everywhere, swiftly opening to reveal their full glory. The blooms would fade all too quickly, but would leave behind a womb full of seeds that in time would renew the cycle. When the seeds were mature, the womb would split open, returning them to the earth. Then new roots would sprout and new branches rise toward the sky. Life and death. Beginnings and endings. One always led to the other.

Tanner was a man of vision. The blooms were as real to him now as they would be to others in a few more weeks. He closed his eyes, breathing deeply, inhaling the rich scent of earth mixed with the fragrance of roses that for the moment he only imagined.

In his mind's eye he could see the arbor covered with roses, a gleaming, white hammock swinging beneath the bower. Lara lying in his arms as they counted the blossoms surrounding them.

He knew everything about cultivating roses. He knew that he could make the rose-covered arbor a reality. The hammock, too. That would just be a matter of making a simple purchase. But he didn't have the slightest idea how to go about getting Lara back into his arms.

Soybeans, wheat and rice, like the roses, were easy to grow as long as the weather cooperated. The labor was hard, and it was a challenge to stay up on the latest technology, but the fundamentals remained the same. He knew when and how to plant the seeds, fertilize the crops and reap the harvest. He even knew how to compensate for the things that were beyond his control, like heat and rain.

But love... He was beginning to realize he didn't know a damn thing. Not even where to start. As the light of day grew dim, Tanner reluctantly turned his back on his garden and returned to the house. A quick shower washed away the sweat and the dirt, then he found himself pacing restlessly again.

No, he decided, he didn't have to worry about depression. Depression meant sitting still, moping. Shock, denial and anger he was more than capable of, but he had too much energy to stay depressed.

Again he turned to work as a cure, reconstructing the living room as he had the garden. The barren space was intolerable. Its cold, impersonal walls reminding him once more of a funeral parlor. He went to the basement and began to resurrect the odd pieces that had been relegated to its dark recesses over the years.

An old, camelback sofa replaced the leather couch. A wing chair stood in for the deceased recliner. The wooden rocker that had been his grandmother's favorite was placed in front of the window where she used to watch the world go by.

A brass-trimmed trunk that he'd taken off to college and a vintage, foot-powered sewing machine replaced the teak occasional tables that had been fuel for the blaze.

Framed, black-and-white family photos were rescued from a box of paraphernalia and hung on the wall. A homemade rag rug was unrolled on the hardwood floors. The duck decoys carved by Grandpa McElroy were restored to the mantel where Jodi's pottery pieces had briefly reigned.

Slowly the room began to resemble the place he had loved to visit as a child. As he put the finishing touches in place—a crystal vase, a painting by his mother— Tanner admired his handiwork. The sofa and chair needed new fabric, the rocker could stand a refinishing, but at last the house he had lived in for years truly felt like home.

If Lara saw any ghosts here now, they could only be those of the departed family members standing awkwardly in the photos, returning for an earthly visit. He smiled, remembering Great-Uncle Henry, the terrible specter who had slammed doors and broken Grandmother's china when he and Samantha were children.

Jodi didn't live here anymore.

Exhausted but pleased with himself, he eased into the rocker and watched the sun kiss the earth good-night. Soon a star appeared, to be joined by another and another until the sky was filled with bright points of light. He wondered if Lara was looking at the same stars, if she was thinking about him. Had she made a wish on that first star, too?

Wishes. If wishes were horses . . .

There had to be more that he could do. He hadn't sat idly this summer, when the drought had singed the country and threatened to steal his crops. He had fought back with everything he had, every ounce of water he could squeeze from the earth. There had to be something he could do now.

But Tanner was mystified when it came to the female of the species. If he was to have any hope of getting Lara back, he needed help. Samantha was his first thought, but his older sister's advice usually came with a heavy dose of, "If you had listened to me in the first place . . ." He could definitely live without that.

He wondered what Hank was planning to do to get Susan back. There was one sure way to find out. With a swift glance at his watch to make sure it wasn't too late, Tanner picked up the phone and called his old buddy.

Hank answered so quickly, Tanner was sure he had been waiting by the phone. His disappointed, "Oh, it's you," confirmed Tanner's suspicion that Hank had been hoping for a call from someone else.

"I love you, too," he chided his old friend.

"Sorry," Hank said. "I was kind of hoping you were Susan."

"So I figured. How are things going on the home front?"

"Not so good. She won't even let me in the house or stay on the phone long enough for me to tell her that I'll go along with this stupid idea of Lara's." When Tanner cleared his throat threateningly, Hank hurried to add, "Nothing against Lara personally. I would just rather be sleeping in my own bed with my own wife."

"As opposed to sleeping in someone else's bed with someone else's wife?" Tanner asked.

"No!" Hank denied vehemently. "Hellfire, why does everybody have to keep turning everything I say against me? You know darned well that's not what I meant."

"No offense, Hank," Tanner soothed, "but you'd better be careful if you're handing your wife loaded statements like that one. She's liable to wind up giving you a backside full of buckshot."

"I know, I know. But what's a guy supposed to do? Susan has the way with words. I never could say two sentences without sticking my foot in my mouth."

"Maybe you should concentrate on nonverbal communication then," Tanner suggested.

"Wouldn't I like to!"

"That's not what I meant," Tanner said firmly, "although I admit that's what I would prefer, too. Unfortunately, women are apt to have different ideas."

"Yeah, they're full of wild ideas," Hank agreed. "But what's a guy going to do? It may be tough living with them, but it sure as hell is lonely without them."

"Amen," Tanner agreed with feeling.

"So what did you call for, anyway?" Hank asked. "I don't want to tie up the line, just in case."

"Believe it or not, I was hoping to get some advice."

"About women? From me? Son, you must be hurting!"

"Hurting isn't the word. I'm dying. I really screwed things up with Lara, and now I've got to figure out a way to set them straight again."

"Well, I wish I could help, Tanner, but any advice I give you is bound to be wrong."

"You don't have some kind of plan for getting Susan back?"

"If I did, do you think I'd still be sitting here, talking to you?"

"No, I guess not. Well, thanks, anyway. I'll keep—"

"Wait a second," Hank interrupted. "Maybe I do have an idea."

"What is it?" Tanner was dubious.

Hank ignored Tanner's lack of confidence. "Why don't you call Susan?" he said.

"What?"

"Yeah! You call Susan and ask her what to do about Lara. They've been friends for years. She'll know what you should do. Women are always better at these heart things, anyway."

Tanner considered it carefully for a second and then admitted slowly, "You know, that might not be such a bad idea."

"Hell," Hank swore, "it's a great idea!" He paused for a second, then added slyly, "And Tanner?"

"Yes?"

"If she does give you any advice, be sure and let me know what it is. Okay?"

Tanner slapped his thigh with a wry laugh. "I should have known there was something in this for you."

"Hey, it's a tough world, son. We men have to stick together."

"All for one and one for all?"

"To the end, old son, to the very end."

Tanner hung up, feeling better. He was still floundering, but not without hope. Knowing he wasn't in the life raft alone was some comfort. Taking a deep breath, he picked up the phone and dialed his second SOS.

Susan Metcalf answered her phone in the middle of the first ring. "I told you not to call me anymore, Hank Metcalf!" she shouted, then the phone was slammed back onto the hook.

Tanner winced and jiggled his ear with one index finger to subdue the echo that was sounding against his eardrum. Hank was right; things were not going well for him and his wife.

Tanner dialed the number again, placing the speaking end of the receiver against his mouth and holding the listening end as far away as possible.

"Damn it! How many times—?"

"This isn't Hank, it's Tanner!" he shouted, hoping she had been able to hear him over her own voice before she slammed the phone down again. Things weren't going at all well for Hank.

Three strikes and you're out, he told himself as he dialed the Metcalf residence once more.

"This better not be you, Hank," Susan warned right off the bat, but didn't hang up.

"It isn't, it's Tanner!" he replied quickly.

There was a slight pause, then he heard his name repeated suspiciously. "Tanner?"

"Tanner McNeil," he clarified unnecessarily.

"If Hank asked you to call for him . . ."

"No, no," he assured her. "At least not for the reason you think."

"What's that supposed to mean?"

"Well, Hank did suggest I call you," Tanner admitted, then rushing on before she could hang up again, "but not for him—for me."

"Excuse me?" Susan inquired.

"Hank said you might be able to help me. With Lara, I mean."

There was a long pause before she asked, "Why do you need help with Lara? What have you done to her?"

"I didn't do anything to her!" Tanner protested. "She's just a little . . . upset with me."

"Does she have reason to be upset?" Susan asked.

"Well, yes, Lara probably thinks she does."

"Well, then I'd say she probably thinks right. Honestly, I don't know why women put up with men."

"I know, I know. We're a bunch of sorry bastards. Or at least this bastard is sorry, and he would really like to make it up to the b . . . er, the woman in question."

"Nice catch," she congratulated.

Tanner grinned. At least Susan hadn't lost her sense of humor. That was a good sign, for both Hank and himself.

"Thank you. Now how about it? Do you think you can help me out?"

"I don't know. What exactly was the nature of this error you made?"

"I, uh, got her confused with someone else."

"Jodi?"

"Yes."

"Are we talking the wrong name in a moment of passion or something worse?" she asked.

Tanner gulped hard. "Worse."

"Boy, you are in trouble."

He winced uncomfortably. She was right.

"Don't panic, now, a save isn't out of the question. Yet." Susan was taking pity on him, Tanner realized.

"You'll help, then?"

"If I can. Why don't you tell me the whole story?"

"Well," Tanner began, but came to an immediate stop. "Maybe you should come over here. I think it might make things a little clearer."

There was a pause before she asked suspiciously, "Are you there alone?"

"Nobody here but us chickens." Tanner sensed she was leaning toward a refusal so he tipped the scales with a heartfelt "Please, Susan."

THIRTY MINUTES LATER Tanner opened the door and ushered in not only Susan Metcalf, but Kelly Ryan, as well.

"I thought we might need a little extra brain tissue on this one," Susan offered as an explanation for Kelly's presence.

"Things sound that bad to you?" he asked in dismay.

"I think we will reserve judgment until you've told us the full story," Susan hedged, craning her neck to one side, peering around the doorways leading off the entry.

"Relax," Tanner told her. "Hank isn't here."

Susan colored guiltily. "Sorry, I just thought he might have put you up to something."

"Well, he didn't. Although I have to tell you, I'm on his side. I always thought it was a mistake for you guys to break up," Tanner said without apology.

"Yes, well, you don't know all the facts, or you might think differently." When Tanner started to speak, she held her hands up in front of her, palms facing him, signaling a standoff. "No, I'm not going to tell you. We came to hear your sad story, not mine."

"That's right," Kelly chimed in, backing her up, "and don't leave out any details."

"Okay." Tanner sighed. He led them into the living room, giving the women the couch and settling himself in the wing chair. He studied the expectant looks on Kelly's and Susan's faces, trying to decide exactly where to start.

"Look around this room and tell me who you see," he finally told them.

Both women turned their heads, taking in the family heirlooms that he had placed there just a few hours earlier. Then they turned to look at each other with blank expressions.

Kelly finally spoke for them. "We're not sure what you mean. I mean, aside from us and the pictures of your family we don't see anyone."

Tanner nodded, satisfied with the confirmation of his efforts to eradicate Jodi's presence. "Yesterday," he explained to them, "Lara stood in this same room and saw Jodi."

"Jodi was here?" they asked simultaneously.

"Only in spirit," he said. "Yesterday all this stuff was in the basement. This room was filled with pictures and mementos of Jodi's travels. With furniture that I guess I had subconsciously chosen to please her. Lara saw all that and concluded that I really hadn't put Jodi out of my life yet, and that until I did, there wouldn't be room for her."

"Was she right?" asked Susan.

"At the time, probably. But I denied it, of course." Tanner leaned forward, bracing his elbows on his knees, steepling his fingers.

"From the first time Lara and I got together, I have been trying to push her into marriage, and she's been trying to force me to slow down."

"Well, that is kind of rushing it, don't you think?" Susan suggested. "You have been seeing each other for only a couple of months at the most. What's the hurry?"

"You sound just like Lara," Tanner groaned. "She kept telling me that we hadn't had time to get to know each other, and that I hadn't had enough time to get over my breakup with Jodi to be getting involved so seriously with her. Yesterday, when she came in here and saw all of Jodi's things, she became more sure than ever that she was right."

"And you said . . ." Kelly encouraged, when Tanner paused for a long, silent moment.

He took a deep breath and let it out slowly. "I accused her of being just like Jodi. Unable to make a commitment. Unable to settle down. Always looking for something better somewhere else, while she kept me dangling on the hook."

"Oh," Susan murmured. "Oh, boy."

Kelly began to whistle tunelessly.

"I was angry," Tanner defended himself. "A man can only take so much rejection, you know."

The women sat silently for what seemed to Tanner like an unbearable length of time. Finally Susan spoke again. "Do you really believe Lara is like Jodi, unable to make a commitment?"

"Hell, no!" he exclaimed. "I may be a little thick at times, but I'm not stupid. Anyone who could stick out three years of law school and then leave the security of a big firm for her own practice has to be capable of commitment."

Kelly nodded approval of his answer, then asked, "Do you really believe Lara is just holding you off, so she can keep her options open?"

"No," Tanner denied harshly. He hadn't been expecting a Southern females' version of the Spanish Inquisition. When the women just arched their eyebrows and waited, he continued uncomfortably. "I realize now that having handled several divorces and having been through one herself, Lara knows what it takes for a person to fully recover from a broken relationship."

He stood restlessly and walked over to the fireplace, shifting his weight awkwardly from his heels to his toes and back again. "I didn't want to admit she was right. That breaking up with Jodi had affected me more than I realized."

"But you do realize it now?" Kelly asked.

"Yes."

Susan continued the cross-examination. "And just what led you to this revelation?"

Tanner studied his hands carefully, vaguely noticing that he still had a bit of dirt and ashes beneath his fingernails. He turned his back toward the women and said, almost in a whisper, "I burned everything."

"You what?" they asked in unison.

He closed his eyes and pressed his lips tightly together, gathering his courage. When he turned to face them again, it was with the humility and genuine remorse of a schoolboy confessing to his teacher.

"I burned everything," he repeated. "Everything that was in this room yesterday, everything that reminded me of Jodi. I burned it all." And then he told them the whole story.

THE OLD GRANDFATHER CLOCK in the entry was striking midnight when Susan and Kelly finally left.

"Do you really think you can get her to come back out here?" Tanner asked them once more as he walked between them toward Kelly's car.

"We'll give it our very best shot," Susan promised.

"Just don't forget your part," Kelly added.

"You really think that will work?" he asked dubiously.

"It will, if you're honest with her," Susan answered. "Just tell her everything, just like you told us."

"And don't push," Kelly warned him. "If she needs time to think, give it to her. If she wants to take things slow, then make like a turtle. Understand?"

Tanner nodded. "Yes, ma'am. I understand." He put an arm around each of them, squeezing their shoulders affectionately. "I can't tell you both how much I appreciate this."

"No problem," Susan said with a smile. "That's what friends are for."

"Besides," Kelly reminded him with a grin, "we are not doing this for nothing. You're going to owe us. Big time."

"Don't worry," he assured them, "you'll be repaid in full, with interest. Just name the favor. If you can get Lara to give me a second chance, you can name your own reward."

He watched them pull away, sending a thousand prayers with them. Then he switched off the porch light and took himself upstairs to bed, a naked body on a bare mattress.

Tomorrow he would have to run in to town for new sheets and maybe some flowers to fill the crystal vase in the living room, Tanner thought sleepily. He would have to go early, so he could be back in plenty of time.

He refused to even consider the possibility that Lara wouldn't come. He had two of the best minds in Morristown working overtime on his behalf. This plan had to succeed.

9

Mornings were never easy for Lara. This particular Monday morning was the most difficult she could remember in ages. She had wallowed in self-pity on Sunday, never bothering to get dressed. She'd decided there was no point, when she was only going from her bed to the refrigerator and back again.

But Monday was a different story. She had a practice to run. Advice to give. Bills to pay. There was no time for self-pity. She made herself get up and put on her favorite power suit, the navy-blue pinstripe she usually reserved for the courtroom. Then she swallowed a pot of coffee—extrastrength—and trudged out to her car, briefcase in hand.

The briefcase usually rode shotgun, but this morning its spot had already been commandeered by a leafless, thorny rosebush. Lara grabbed the culprit quickly and flung it out and onto the pavement.

Her first instinct was to crush it beneath her tires like a venomous snake. She jumped into the car and spurred it into Reverse, intending to do just that, but her Mercedes balked, refusing to cooperate.

Lara got back out and stared at the bush, debating over a more suitable demise for the undesirable creature. Reluctantly she extended two dainty fingers and lifted it by one scraggly twig. Lips pursed in disgust, she hauled it off to the front porch, until its fate could be decided at a more convenient time.

The Mercedes, the Jezebel, performed beautifully after its path had been cleared and Lara found herself at the office without further delay. Not that it would have mattered if she'd been late. By 9:00 a.m. two of her appointments, her only two for the day, had been canceled. The deposition she'd expected to last all afternoon had been completed in half an hour.

Of course, there was plenty to do; there always was around the office. Busywork. She could finish summarizing the depositions she had taken last week. She could sift through her billing records and figure out who was going to get nasty Pay Me Now letters in the mail this week. She could even—horrors—clean out her desk drawers.

But Lara wasn't really in the mood for doing busywork. Those types of things were best saved for days when she had boundless energy that needed to be used up. They weren't at all suitable for a day when she desperately needed a distraction, some scintillating new case to keep her from crawling back into bed and yanking the covers over her head.

At three-thirty she found herself across the street at Riley's, sipping her fifteenth cup of coffee, trying not to remember that first, lengthy conversation she had had with Tanner. Actually, if memory served, it had been a story hour. To be considered conversation, both people had to talk.

She and Tanner really hadn't had any conversation. They had had body language and pillow talks. They had had accusations and innuendos. They had had an out-and-out, major screamfest. But they had never really just had an everyday conversation.

Well, maybe once. When she had called to ask him out for New Year's Eve. Maybe even twice, if she counted the Valentine's dinner. And technically she supposed she could include Saturday, before Hank had arrived. Before the screamfest.

She set down her coffee on the table and idly began to circle the rim with her finger. Outside the sun was shining, and it looked as if they might be in for an early spring, after all. She wondered if Tanner was working in the wheat field, checking the hundred acres he had shown her. Or maybe he would be in one of the other fields, getting them ready for the rice and soybeans he would plant in April.

April. It seemed so far away. Six weeks. The same amount of time she had been seeing Tanner. Who would have guessed so much could happen in such a short period?

Lara took another sip, grimacing slightly when she realized her coffee had grown cold. She lifted her head to signal Pat Riley for a refill, smiling politely while he topped up her mug.

A young man on a stool at the bar caught her attention, or rather his backpack did. Was he a traveler like Jodi, going wherever his feet could take him?

What sort of people carried their whole lives on their backs? she wondered. What sort of person was content to roam the earth with no particular place to call home?

She had wanted to travel that way when she finished college—footloose and free, without a care in the world. But she had gotten a scholarship to law school, and her family would never have understood if she had turned it down. She didn't regret not going.

Did Jodi regret not staying?

Lara looked out the window as she heard the cry of a mockingbird, perched on a leafless branch outside. Soon other birds would be returning, building nests for their eggs. The trees would be full and green. Spring was just around the corner and summer not far behind. Would either bring Jodi with them?

"Lara!"

She jerked around as she heard her name, relaxing when she saw Kelly and Susan walking toward her table.

"Well, hello," she greeted them. "Come have a seat."

Her two friends hurried to comply, scooting onto the bench on the opposite side of the table.

"Playing hooky?" Kelly asked her. "I thought they didn't let you lawyers out until after five."

"Time off for good behavior," Lara pleaded.

"Well, great. Susan and I were just about to treat ourselves to the specialty of the house. You might as well pig out with us."

"Oh, no," Lara moaned. "Not death by chocolate!"

"It's the only way to go," Susan assured her.

Pat Riley laughed, he'd plainly overheard them. "Come on, Lara. Order one, too, or they'll torture you by making you watch as they eat theirs."

"All right," she said, surrendering. "Make it three."

"Attagirl." Kelly beamed. "We'll run every size eight out of this town yet."

"Forget the eights," Lara told her as Pat set their orders in front of them. "By the time we finish these, we'll be scaring away the tens."

She could already feel her skirt tightening as she dug her spoon into the luscious dessert. Three scoops of chocolate chunk ice cream, sitting on a pecan brownie throne, drenched in hot fudge, topped with whipped cream and chocolate sprinkles and crowned with a chocolate-covered cherry. It was good enough to die for, she decided after the first bite.

After a cautious glance at her coconspirator, Susan abandoned her sundae for a moment and began to set their plan in motion. "So, Lara," she began innocently, "how's your love life?"

The lawyer choked on a piece of brownie and quickly grabbed the glass of water Pat had brought with her ice cream.

"Goodness, are you okay?" asked Kelly.

"Fine, fine." Lara coughed weakly. "You just surprised me, that's all."

"Didn't you tell me Friday that you had been seeing Tanner McNeil?" Susan continued.

"Make that 'was,' as in past tense. Things didn't work out."

"Oh, that's too bad," Kelly sympathized. "I thought you two were going to be perfect together. What happened?"

Lara carefully wiped the chocolate off her mouth, pushing the unfinished dessert away from her. Maybe her skirt wasn't in danger, after all. Her appetite had suddenly vanished. "Same old song, different verse. Right man, right place, wrong time."

"What was wrong with the timing?" asked Susan.

"Tanner isn't ready for another serious relationship."

Kelly took in the shimmer in Lara's eyes that didn't quite match her matter-of-fact expression. "Is that your opinion or his?"

"Well, mine actually."

"Based on?" Susan prodded.

"Oh, a lot of things," Lara said evasively. Both her friends pushed their half-eaten desserts to one side along with hers, leaning forward, elbows on the table. Clearly they weren't going to do the polite thing and let the subject drop. Some friends.

"Go on," Kelly encouraged her. "We're listening."

"No, I don't want to bore you with the details."

"We'll let you know when it gets boring," Susan assured her.

Lara was tempted to disappear into the ladies' room and climb out the window. Then she remembered that Riley's ladies' room didn't have a window.

She could just tell her friends it was none of their business, which was true, but she had never been a secretive person. Her life was an open book to almost anyone.

Carefully she searched for a brief explanation that would satisfy her friends. "On the one hand," she said, "Tanner doesn't want to discuss Jodi or acknowledge that she still exists."

"And on the other hand?" Kelly inquired.

"On the other hand, his house is still filled with her things, and—" She broke off suddenly, without finishing the sentence.

"And what?" Susan asked, when Lara didn't continue.

"And whenever we disagree, Tanner accuses me of being just like her."

Kelly and Susan exchanged knowing glances. Kelly reached out and gently covered Lara's hand with hers.

"I know that must be hard to take, but don't you think you might be able to work through that? So Tanner has some old battle scars that act up now and then. Are they really severe enough for you to give up on him? I'm sure that eventually they will fade away."

"Not until the bullet is removed."

"You mean Jodi's things? Just ask Tanner to get rid of them," Susan suggested.

But Lara flipped her hand as if to shoo away a pesky fly. "No, those are just trivial things. I mean, every time Jodi comes back she'll reopen those old wounds. And if she came back to stay, well, that would kill our relationship for sure."

"But who says Jodi is coming back?" Kelly wanted to know.

"Jodi says, that's who," Lara replied. "She sent him a postcard from Mexico, saying that she would be back this summer, just like she promised."

This time her friends shared a look of surprise. Susan fumbled for a moment, then asked, "Did Tanner show you this postcard?"

"Not exactly. I sort of found it lying around the kitchen. But that's beside the point, which is that he led me to believe it was all over between them, when it wasn't."

Susan and Kelly sat in an awkward silence. Lara unwittingly gave them the opportunity to discuss this new development by scrambling out of the booth and dashing off to the rest room with a hastily mumbled, "Excuse me."

"Well?" Susan asked, the moment Lara was out of hearing.

"Well, what?"

"Don't be stupid. It doesn't suit you. Do we go on with the plan or not?"

"I don't know. You're the one who got us into this," Kelly complained. "You decide."

"Damn!" Susan muttered. "Why didn't Tanner tell us Jodi was coming back?"

"Maybe he doesn't believe she will," Kelly suggested.

"Or maybe he doesn't care if she does," Susan added.

Kelly considered that for a moment, then asked, "Do you really think he's that sure about his feelings?"

"For Jodi or for Lara?"

"For both of them."

Susan reached out and pulled her slowly melting sundae back in front of her, obviously thinking the subject over carefully as the rich, smooth chocolate slid down her throat, reaching an answer just as the last bit of brownie disappeared.

"I don't think any man would bare his soul like Tanner did last night, unless he was sure about his feelings . . . for both Jodi and Lara," she clarified, before Kelly could get the question out. "I think Tanner didn't mention the postcard because he forgot about it. It doesn't matter if Jodi comes back or not. He doesn't care anymore."

"All right," Kelly said. "I'll agree. So do we go on with the plan?"

"Yes, but it's going to be Plan B."

"I didn't know we had a Plan B."

"We do now," Susan announced.

"Well, quick, tell me what it is. Lara's coming back."

"It's called honesty."

"I'm sorry, I didn't catch that," Lara apologized as she took her seat again.

Susan took a deep breath. "I said, it's time we were honest with you."

"I don't understand," Lara said. "Honest about what?"

"Tanner."

Lara shook her head in confusion. "I don't know what you mean."

"Tanner called me last night to ask for advice on how to get you back. Kelly and I went over and talked to him. Or listened to him, actually. For hours. He told us all about his feelings for Jodi and for you."

"Well that's more than he has told me!" Lara exclaimed angrily. "Why did you two come in here and pretend not to know anything?"

"We're sorry," Kelly told her quickly. "We were just trying to make sure we knew both sides of the story, before we put the plan to work."

"What plan?" Lara asked.

"Tanner wanted us to convince you to give him a second chance," Susan said. "Kelly and I decided to see if his story checked out first and then, if it did, we would get you to go out and see him."

"And just how did you plan to accomplish that? Or dare I ask?"

Kelly winced at her friend's rising anger. "Lara, we just wanted to help. Give Cupid a little boost."

"I wouldn't mind giving you a little boost right now," Lara threatened. "What exactly was your plan?"

Sheepishly Susan gave her the basics. "We were going to tell you that Tanner had started hitting the bottle again, only worse than ever. That we thought he might even be suicidal, and that you might be able to prevent something tragic happening."

"And is there any truth to all that?" Lara demanded.

"No," the conspirators whispered.

"So why didn't you go through with it?"

At Susan's nod, Kelly told Lara, "Tanner didn't mention the postcard or Jodi coming back. That caught us by surprise."

"I see," Lara said, "and that made you decide to come clean and forgo the blatant manipulation."

Susan shook her head. "We are not telling you all this now, just so we can sleep better. We think that Tanner left out that fact because he really doesn't care if Jodi comes back. You're the woman he cares about now, and we think—" she paused "—we hope—that you'll reconsider and give him a chance to tell you what he told us."

"No, thanks," Lara replied. "I may be a fool when it comes to men, but I'm not a glutton for punishment." Opening her purse, she pulled out some money for her share of the tab and flung it onto the table. "Do me a favor, girls. Don't do me any more favors."

"Wait," Susan pleaded, grabbing one handle of Lara's bag before she could walk away. "I don't blame you for being mad at us, but if you won't take our advice, then at least take your own."

"And what would that be?" she asked wearily.

"Don't make rash decisions before you fully explore all the possibilities. It was good advice when you gave it to me. I hope you'll at least consider taking it yourself."

Lara hesitated, feeling her anger fade.

"What exactly did Tanner tell you?" she asked them.

"No, I think we've said and done enough," Kelly answered. "Just go listen to him, Lara. Make up your own mind, and we promise we won't interfere again."

Susan let go of the purse handle. "We both promise."

Lara looked at their earnest faces. They were two of her oldest and dearest friends. Neither had ever let her down. "I'll think about it," she told them, relenting, "but I'm not promising anything."

She walked briskly down the street to the Mercedes and headed for home, arguing the entire way about whether to go see Tanner or not. When she came to a stop at Harold's Corner, her car seemed once again to develop a mind of its own, turning left instead of right as it was supposed to.

Oh, whom was she kidding? The car hadn't steered itself any more than a Ouija board did. Each simply responded to the will of the person guiding it. *Better go to Tanner's now and be done with it*, she told herself.

Two blocks later she changed her mind again and made an illegal U-turn that would take her back toward home. Ten minutes later she pulled into her driveway and switched the Mercedes off. There, that hadn't been so difficult. She was home and she would stay here if she had any sense at all.

But she had forgotten the wily rosebush. It ambushed her again at the front door, snagging her last, nail-polish-free pair of hose. Blasted creature. She bent to recapture the villain, determined to be rid of it once and for all. The bush seemed to have other ideas, though.

The instant her fingers touched it, the thorny bush pricked her heart and the memories came flooding back. "Love is the root from which passion springs," she heard the wind whisper. "Though it may seem barren through the winter, it will branch out again each spring."

Could she turn her back on the man who had spoken those words? Could she give him up so easily? She had told Susan she wasn't a fool. Why was she acting like one?

A rose didn't grow all by itself. Or if it did, it would never be able to reach its full potential. It had to be nurtured and cared for. She stared again at the bare root she held in her hand. It would never bloom at all, if it wasn't planted first.

She hurried back to the Mercedes, bringing Tanner's rosebush with her. This time the car continued in one direction, with no indecisive U-turns to slow it down.

TANNER HAD BEEN WAITING impatiently all afternoon. He knew Susan and Kelly wouldn't be able to talk to her until Kelly got out of school, but it didn't keep him from staring at the gravel road, willing Lara's car to appear.

He paced back and forth in the room, sat in the rocker, then paced some more. Alternating back and forth. Pacing and rocking, slowly going insane with fear. What if she refused to come? He had left it to the girls to come up with an excuse to bring her out here.

"Tell her anything," he'd told them. "Tell her I'm desperate. Tell her I love her. Just get her to listen to me."

What if they couldn't convince her? What if she just didn't care anymore? But that was impossible. Lara was right; passion was only part of a relationship, but he knew that the kind of passion existing between them could only spring from a source much deeper than the desire for physical satisfaction.

Lara loved him. She had to.

When he finally heard her Mercedes purr to a stop, he panicked. She was here. Now what did he do? Where did he start? What should he say? What if he said the wrong thing? Again. How many second chances was one man entitled to?

"Just tell her everything, just like you told us," the girls had said. They had been smart enough to figure out a way to get Lara back to the farm. Their advice was probably the best he could have gotten. He was going to owe Hank big time, too. If this worked.

Tanner took a quick peek out the window, just to be sure it was her. It was. Lord, she was beautiful. Quickly he wiped his damp palms on his jeans and ran trembling fingers through his hair. Maybe he should have worn a suit. Damn, there wasn't time to change now. Besides, this was what she was used to seeing him in, anyway.

He placed his hands on the doorknob, closed his eyes and inhaled deeply to steady himself before opening the door. Lara had just reached the first step when he walked out onto the porch.

She stopped immediately, looking up at him. "Hello, Tanner," she whispered huskily. "The girls said you wanted to see me."

He knew that they had to have said a lot more than that for her to be here, but didn't press the point. She was here. That was all that mattered.

"I want to apologize for all the things I said to you the other day. I know that doesn't excuse the way I behaved. I hope you'll give me a chance to set things right."

She licked her lips nervously. "I don't know if they can be set right. But if you're ready to talk, I'll listen. As I recall, you owe me a story hour."

He felt his mouth twitch slightly with a smile. He had almost forgotten that morning they had sat in the café and she had told him about Kevin. And after they had left Riley's, he had kissed her for the first time. It seemed so long ago. So hard to imagine that there had ever been a first kiss or a time when he had never kissed Lara at all. She was so much a part of his life now.

"I think it's time I repaid you, then. Come inside where we can talk."

She followed him in, noticing the way they both seemed to fastidiously avoid touching. It seemed strange, after all the times they had spent doing nothing but touch each other, everywhere, every way there was.

Enough of that, she told herself, snapping sharply back to attention. *Listen, but don't touch. Look, but—*

Whatever her next thought was going to be, the shock of seeing the transformed living room forever deleted it from her mind. It was gone. Everything was gone. Jodi had been removed.

She turned to stare blankly at Tanner. "What...? Where...?" she stammered, not understanding. "Why...?"

"Please, Lara, sit down. I'll explain everything."

It pleased him for some reason that she chose the rocker. All his life he had seen the women who had loved him sitting there, watching him with loving smiles. His mother. His grandmother. It was easy to imagine Lara sitting there for the next fifty years. Rocking their children. Their grandchildren.

But he was getting ahead of himself. He put a firm brake on those thoughts, pushing them to the back of his mind until a later, more appropriate time.

"I'm listening," he heard her say.

His mouth felt parched. A drink, a strong drink, would have gone down very well. But he resisted the temptation. He didn't want Lara to have any doubt that he was thinking clearly.

"Sorry," he said, apologizing for his delay, "I don't know where to start."

"The beginning is usually best. Tell me about you and Jodi. How did you meet? What attracted you to each other?"

Tanner walked around the room as he talked, turning away when the story became difficult, staring her in the eye when he wanted to be sure a point got across.

"Jodi and I met our first year in college. A world history class. I guess there was no great mystery about the initial attraction. She was a pretty, long-legged blonde. I was your typical, horny freshman. It was lust at first sight."

"Just lust?" Lara asked skeptically.

"Yes, at first," Tanner said with certainty. "We dated off and on through college. Nothing really happened to test our relationship. We never fought. There were no major issues between us. We just sort of drifted along.

"I majored in agriculture. She majored in languages. We both minored in history. I guess that was something we had in common, at least. A love for the past. I know it sounds as if we were incredibly naive, but neither of us spent much time thinking of the future. We were just enjoying being kids.

"Then all of a sudden we were seniors. School was almost over, and the real world was waiting just on the horizon. We began to see each other exclusively. I began to think about what I wanted to do. Grandma and Grandpa McElroy had offered to let me take over the farm. I had been working here on summers and weekends. No one else in the family had any interest in the place, and I knew it was work I enjoyed, so I accepted."

"How did Jodi feel about the prospect of being a farmer's wife?" Lara asked him.

"She never really said one way or the other. She was happy for me, because she knew I loved being outside, growing things. She wasn't the kind of person who wanted to be chained to a desk, either. I think we both just assumed that she would settle down as easily as I would."

Lara studied him carefully, trying to read the man as she listened to his story. "But she ended up traveling instead. How did that happen?"

"It started out as one last hurrah. One of my cousins agreed to work on the farm the summer after I graduated, so Jodi and I could enjoy one last season of irresponsibility. We wanted to backpack Europe, but we didn't have the money to get there."

Lara smiled. "I guess every college kid has dreams of hitting the high road to Scotland at some point. Earlier today I was remembering my own plans to do that right after college."

"Why didn't you go?"

"Law school. I got a scholarship, and one of the requirements was that I spend the summer clerking for a judge. But go on," she urged him. "You couldn't go to Europe, so what did you do?"

"We walked all the way to the West Coast. Saw California and Mexico. It was a great experience. But, like I've told Jodi a hundred times, it was the once-in-a-lifetime variety for me."

"You don't want to travel anymore?" she asked.

"Oh, I'd love to travel. Someday I would love to see Europe. Car trips, train trips, plane trips, a cruise. I'll travel anyway, just so long as I don't have to walk. And when I get there, I want to sleep in a nice, warm bed, take hot showers and eat food that isn't cold out of a can."

"Those sound like reasonable stipulations," Lara agreed.

Tanner shook his head. "Jodi didn't think so. Roughing it was part of the adventure for her. She loved it. So much that she didn't want to give it up. She came back here with me in the fall, but she didn't stay. She wanted to make just one more trip before she settled down. Jodi took off again on her own, promising she would be back the next summer.

"She did come back," he continued. "But she was already growing restless, anxious to see more places. She left again in the fall, swearing she needed just one more trip. That's the way it's been ever since. Except that each year she came back later and left sooner. Finally, last summer she didn't show up at all."

Lara rocked back and forth in an even tempo. Listening, thinking, remembering. "But didn't she come back in October?"

"Yes." Tanner nodded. "I hadn't heard from her in months. Usually she would send postcards. Occasionally I would get a package with some kind of trinket in it. But the whole summer went by without my hearing from her this time. Then one day she showed up out of the blue.

"I had had it by then. I guess we both knew we had reached the limits. You were right about the furniture, about this whole room. I fixed it up last winter. I guess I was trying to show her the house could be the kind of home she might enjoy, if she just gave it a chance. She never even saw it."

Tanner walked over to stand beside Lara's chair, staring out the window. "I was working in that field over there," he said, pointing across the road. "Way down at the end. I was trying to turn it under, after it had been burned off. The tractor broke down. I was trying to fix it, when she showed up."

"What happened?" Lara asked him. "Why didn't she stay?"

"I told her not to," he said simply. "I couldn't take it anymore. For months I had been thinking she was dead or hurt somewhere, and I would never know. All of a sudden she shows up without a scratch on her. 'I'm sorry.' That's all she could say. 'I'm sorry.'" He shook his head, still not able to understand Jodi's actions. "I told her that if she wasn't here to stay for good, she should leave, and that's exactly what she did."

"But she said she would be back, didn't she?"

"Yeah, she did," he admitted. "And maybe she will. I can't control her, Lara. Nobody can." Tanner turned away from the window, kneeling down on one knee to look Lara directly in the eye. "Whether or not you and I work things out between us, Lara—and God knows, I hope we do—it is over between Jodi and me.

"I really think we had just gotten to be a habit with each other. It was the perfect relationship for college sweethearts or summer romances. Light, undemanding."

Tanner reached out one hand to gently capture Lara's chin, tilting it up so he could look into her eyes. "I never had anything to compare it to before, Lara. Not until I met you. My feelings for you run as swift and deep as a river. Jodi was just a little stream. Pretty and swift after a rain. Nothing but a trickle the rest of the time. Nothing but dust, when it should have been deepest."

Lara felt a tear spill down her cheek. *Darn it.* He always said the most beautiful, most unexpected things, and they always made her cry.

Tanner leaned forward, gently stealing the tears with his lips. Then he pressed his mouth against the soft shell of her ear and whispered his love for her.

"Give me another chance, Lara. Please. I'll give you all the time in the world. Seven days. Seven months. Seven years. It doesn't matter. Just say you'll give me a chance to prove how much I love you."

He thought he had died and gone to heaven when he felt her arms come around him, holding him tightly. Counting his blessings, with Lara being first among them, he lifted her and traded places so that he was the one sitting in the rocker, holding her.

The creak of the rocker and the ticking of the grandfather clock were all that could be heard for an endless time. The lovers were content for once to simply be near each other. No passion, no arguments. Just love.

10

AFTER A LONG, COMFORTABLE silence, Lara reluctantly raised her head from his chest to place a soft, butterfly kiss on the corner of his mouth. Tanner immediately turned his head to deepen the exchange, kissing her thoroughly.

When the kiss ended, she smiled at him, gently brushing a stray lock of hair from his forehead with a tender touch. Then she pulled herself out of his lap, pressing firm hands against his chest, when he would have hauled her back into his arms.

"I'll be right back," she promised. "Wait here."

Tanner forced himself to stay where he was. His willpower almost deserted him when he heard a car door slam. She couldn't be leaving. Not now.

He heard her footsteps returning. Walking up the steps, across the porch; then she was back again, hands held behind her.

"I brought you something," she whispered.

Tanner waited patiently as she came forward to stand in between his parted legs. She brought her hands out and offered him the rosebush.

He held his breath, automatically reaching out to accept the gift, afraid to guess what it meant. Was this her way of telling him he could keep his love, that she didn't want it? Surely not.

"You told me you would give me both passion and love," Lara reminded him. "I want to offer you the same. I want us to plant this here on the farm, together, as a symbol of what we can have if we are willing to accept the responsibility of keeping it alive and flourishing."

Tanner felt the air rush out of his lungs as he took the rosebush with one hand and captured Lara's wrist in the other. "I know just the place for it."

He led her around the house to the garden he had resurrected. Lara stared at the arbor in disbelief. There was no resemblance to the tumbling structure she had glimpsed briefly the other day. In its stead stood a gleaming, white tower and surrounding it like castle guards were thorny, leafless stick plants identical to the one Tanner held in his hand.

"I can't believe this," Lara whispered, walking toward the whitewashed frame. "The other day, this thing looked like the next breeze would blow it away. Now it's beautiful."

She stepped inside the arbor, giving the new hammock a gentle push. As he heard her laugh with pleasure, Tanner decided that it had been worth the extra ten dollars he had paid the clerk to rummage in the storeroom for the out-of-season purchase.

"Do you have magic elves or something?" Lara asked.

"No, I did it myself. I had to do something constructive after—" He broke off abruptly, not intending to get into that part of the story.

"After what?" Lara asked him. "After our fight Saturday?"

Tanner dug the toe of his boot into the freshly tilled earth surrounding the arbor. "After I destroyed all of Jodi's things," he confessed.

"After...? Oh, Tanner, you didn't!" she cried.

He nodded his head gravely. "I was in a rage after you left. I can't ever remember being that angry in my life. It was easy to take it out on Jodi, on the things that had frightened you away from me."

"Oh, Tanner," Lara moaned. "I never meant for you to do anything like that."

"I know. Lara, don't blame yourself. You were right about my not being completely over Jodi yet," he told her. "Yesterday I realized that I had been a prisoner of grief. For the past few months I have been going through the same phases of mourning I experienced when Dad died. Shock, denial, anger. I've been tormented by all of them and I took my frustration out on you."

He took a step forward, grasping her hands and holding them firmly in his. "Lara, I'm sorry for not listening to you, for pushing too fast, too hard. Please, don't think any of it was your fault. Destroying the reminders of Jodi and the loss of those dreams was my key to freedom."

"But how?"

"After you left Saturday, I grabbed everything of hers out of the house and burned it."

He tightened his grip when Lara gasped in horror. "I was just as shocked by my actions as you are. Believe me. But it was the right thing to do. I had to get rid of all that hate that was building up, before it destroyed me. Before it destroyed us. I wish I had had more self-control, but I needed a release. If it hadn't been this, it would have been something else."

Tanner pulled her hands against his chest, then released them, so that he could encircle her with his arms. "I'm not a violent man, Lara. I know what I did must terrify you. But—"

"Hush," she whispered, placing her fingers over his mouth, "I understand. You'll never have to worry about stumbling across any pictures of Kevin and me, either. I burned them all, too. Just as you did Jodi's things. All I have now is a box full of ashes."

"You saved the ashes?"

"As a reminder, of both the beginning and the end of my first love. I know it sounds a bit maudlin, but . . ."

Tanner laughed. "Not as maudlin as what I did." He spread his arms, gesturing widely towards the garden. "I used Jodi's ashes here. They were tilled into the soil, for the roses."

Lara wasn't surprised. It seemed just the sort of thing her poet farmer would do. "You're such a romantic," she murmured.

"Is that a complaint?"

"I should say not. I love it." She tugged his arms back down to her waist, stepping into the warmth of his embrace. "Don't ever change."

"Do you love me then?" he asked.

"Yes," she whispered. "Yes, Tanner. More than I ever thought was possible."

"Will you marry me?"

It shouldn't have, but the proposal caught her completely off guard.

Seeing the wary look creep back into her eyes, Tanner quickly tried to eliminate her doubts. "I'm not trying to rush you," he swore. "You don't have to answer now. Take all the time you need, as long as you promise to think about it. Just don't say no, Lara."

The fact that he didn't get mad should have been all the proof she needed. And it did reassure her considerably. But Lara was still cautious. "I want to, Tanner. I want nothing more than to marry you. But let's take our time, all right?"

Tanner took care to keep his voice even, weeding out any trace of anger or frustration. "Are you still afraid of Jodi coming back?"

"I'm not afraid," she denied, "I just don't like loose ends that keep threatening to unravel."

"How about a compromise, then? Lawyers are supposed to be big on compromise. We'll get engaged now, but we will postpone the wedding till, oh, let's say April."

She shook her head. Some compromise. Six weeks wasn't even long enough to plan a wedding. "August."

Tanner frowned. He would never last that long. "How about May?"

"How about July?" she countered.

"June," he said. "June is the month for weddings. Let's get married in June."

"All right," she conceded, giving in. "June 30."

"June 1," he came back swiftly.

"June 15, and that's my final offer."

Tanner closed his mouth and thought about it for a second. Four months. He would have to wait a whole four months. He looked at his woman, standing defiantly in front of him with her stubborn, belligerent chin thrust out. He loved that chin.

"All right. June 15," he agreed, swooping down to plant a solid kiss on that adorable chin. Picking her up in his arms, he swung her around, letting out a deafening, "Yee-hah!" Lara hugged his neck, laughing happily as they spun in circles around the arbor, then dropping dizzily into the hammock.

She landed in a sprawl across his body, accepting his kisses eagerly, returning them one for one. The status of her hemline was forgotten entirely until she felt strong, callused fingers exploring the soft curves of her bottom beneath the confines of her nylon, control-top panty hose.

"Tanner!" she scolded, "not out here. What if someone comes?"

"I can guarantee a couple of someones will, if you'll just hush and let me get you out of this blasted pair of hose."

"So much for the romantic," she groused. "I refuse to make out with you in a hammock, where any eyes passing by could see us. Besides," she complained, shivering as the cool air met her exposed flesh, "it is too cold out here."

With a great show of fuss Tanner gave in, letting her scramble out of the hammock's web. She was right. It was cold. And it was getting dark. He had a definite preference for making love to Lara in the warmth and the light of a firelit bedroom. The master bedroom. Their bedroom.

Her efforts at straightening her skirt were completely ignored as Tanner picked her up in his arms, carried her into the house and up the stairs.

Lara thought of making a token protest, but decided not to waste her energy. She had the feeling she was going to need every bit of it in the next few hours.

Tanner had pulled the crisp, new linens back earlier, trying to remain optimistic as he waited for Lara to show up. With infinite care he laid her down, then turned to light the fire he had also prepared, just in case.

"Something tells me you were a Boy Scout," Lara commented dryly.

"Eagle Scout," he confirmed proudly, tugging off his boots. He tossed them carelessly into a corner, sending his socks flying after them, joined quickly by his shirt and pants.

He shook his head sadly as he towered beside the bed, strong and virile and not one bit bothered by his own nudity, only slightly concerned that she wasn't in the same state of undress.

"Honey, I hate to tell you this, but you're getting behind. You were supposed to be taking your clothes off, too," he told her.

Lara rolled her head against the pillow. "But remember how much you love to unwrap presents. I didn't want to deprive you of the pleasure."

"You're so considerate. I can't tell you how much that means to me. However, I think tonight I'm going to give your method a try."

"You rip this suit and the wedding's off," she warned him.

Her words chilled him like a bucket of ice water. "That's not funny, Lara."

The hurt look on his face caught her off guard. "Tanner, I was just teasing. I'm not going to change my mind. I promise."

He ignored the navy-blue pinstripe completely, crushing her beneath his hard, tense body. "You better not," he growled against her mouth. "I couldn't let you go, anyway. You are my life now, Lara. I couldn't survive losing you."

"You won't have to," she whispered earnestly. "I am going to marry you, Tanner McNeil, and our marriage will last."

The suit made it to the floor intact. Her blouse wasn't so lucky. But Lara didn't care. Loving Tanner was the most important thing in the world. Why worry about a few buttons?

His kisses burned across her flesh. Hard, stinging kisses, meant to brand her forever his. She accepted each and every one, returning them in kind.

When the sparks began to fly out of control, Tanner stood on his knees before her, dragging the source of her feminine heat across the mattress to meet its masculine counterpart. Rounded thighs parted, then tightened around his hard, slick flanks.

He took hold of her outstretched arms, lifting her up to meet him, their passion for each other flaming in a single blaze in the center of the bed. As he lifted her hips, she willingly climbed astride him, joining their bodies in a final fierce thrust.

As always, their lovemaking was all-consuming. The intensity that had overwhelmed and threatened others was an essential element in each of them. Finally two equal forces were united. Fire with fire.

After the flames had died down, while the sparks smoldered quietly, Lara lay curled against Tanner's side, idly twisting the sparse curls that decorated his chest. Absently she rubbed her calf over his shin.

"Tanner?" she asked.

"Mmm?" Tanner answered drowsily.

"Do you like Woody Allen movies?"

"What?" It wasn't the sort of post lovemaking conversation he was expecting.

"I asked you if you liked Woody Allen movies," Lara repeated.

"Selectively, yes."

"What does that mean?"

"It means that I'm not crazy about everything the man has done, but I do think some of his work is excellent. Now tell me why you asked."

"I was just curious," she said offhandedly. At least he hadn't said he hated Woody. "I just thought I should know what kind of movies my future husband might like."

He grinned at the word "husband," liking the sound of it on her lips. Liking the possessive she had placed in front of it even more. He was going to be Lara's husband.

"What about Alfred Hitchcock?"

"What? Oh, you mean, do I like his movies? Love them. Especially the ones with Jimmy Stewart."

"Me, too," Lara agreed. "And Cary Grant. I like Cary Grant, too."

"What about John Wayne?"

Lara frowned. "I didn't know he made a Hitchcock movie."

"He didn't. I meant, do you like John Wayne movies?"

"Love them. My dad always let me stay up when one was on the late show. I especially liked the ones with Maureen O'Hara."

"Like *The Quiet Man*. Now that was a great movie."

"What about books?" she asked. "What do you like to read?"

"Oh, a little bit of everything."

"Don't hedge. Name some authors."

"Dick Francis."

"Excellent," she agreed.

"Robert Ludlum."

"I think his last book was his best yet."

"You do?" he asked. "Personally, I liked the *Road to Gandalfo* the best."

"That was great, but it was a complete departure from his usual style."

"I know," Tanner said. "Did you read the note he wrote at the beginning? He said he laughed the entire time he was writing it."

"You read those things, too?" Lara asked, delighted.

"Are you kidding? With the price of books these days, I even read the copyright notice."

"You can always go to the library," she pointed out.

"I guess now is as good a time as any to warn you," Tanner confessed. "I tend to be a tad possessive. For instance, I like to own what I read."

"Me, too. But after we're married, we can share custody and cut our costs in half."

"Or buy twice as many books," he suggested.

"Even better. Tell me who else you read," she begged him. "Besides mystery and suspense."

"Oh, lots of different people. Ann Tyler. John Irving. Garrison Keillor. Richard Adams. Jayne Krentz. Sidney Sheldon."

"Wait a second!" Lara objected. "Jayne Krentz writes romance."

"Oh, well. Yeah, I guess she does."

"You read romance novels!" Lara exclaimed.

"If you ever tell anyone, I'll, I'll . . . I'll tell them you do, too," he threatened.

"But where do you get them?" Lara asked. "Somehow I can't imagine you reading the back of those covers in the middle of a bookstore."

"Samantha," he answered. "When I hit puberty, she started picking out the ones she thought I would like and gave them to me. I think she had some idea about making me a more liberated male."

"That explains it," Lara said, snapping her fingers.

"Explains what?"

"The way you talk. You're always saying the most romantic things."

"You think so, hmm?" he asked, preening like a peacock.

"Definitely. Some of those heroes must have rubbed off on you."

"Well, if any of those books are even partially responsible, I'll shove my pride and start buying my own copies. I guess I owe those authors big time, too."

"What for?" Lara had to laugh.

"For helping me win you over. You really had me scared, woman. I had to call in reinforcements."

"You mean Kelly and Susan?" she asked.

"And Hank and those romance authors and even Samantha, I guess."

"I know how Samantha, Susan, Kelly and Krentz are involved, but what does Hank have to do with us getting back together?"

"I called him first," he said. "It was Hank's idea to phone Susan."

"Wow, you really did call out the guard." Lara was impressed and wasn't above a little preening herself.

"I would have done anything to get you back again. Here in my arms, where you belong."

Lara kissed him soundly, loving him more by the minute. "Keep your pride. I'll buy the romance novels for you myself. Consider them your wedding present."

"Thank you. Anything else you want to know? Favorite color? Hobbies, vices . . . ?"

"What's for dinner?"

"Excuse me?"

Lara enunciated clearly and slowly. "What's for dinner? I'd like to know when and what you're going to feed me. I'm starving."

Tanner thought it over carefully. "Didn't you say something about there being some steaks in the freezer the other day?"

"Yes!" He saw her eyes light up in anticipation. "Steak with baked potatoes and a salad. Sounds perfect. I'll just jump in the shower. Let me know when it's ready."

"You want me to fix it?" he asked, dismayed.

"You can handle it," Lara said, tossing the words over her shoulder as she headed toward the bathroom. "I'm sure any sister who gave her brother romance novels also taught him to cook."

"Have you been talking to Samantha?"

"Nope. It was just a simple deduction, my dear Watson. Elementary."

Despite having drawn KP duty, Tanner grinned as he obediently got dressed and walked downstairs to the kitchen. He liked Arthur Conan Doyle, too.

Lara appeared in his bathrobe just as he finished tossing the salads. Together they sat down at the table and fed their famished bodies.

When the edge had been taken off their hunger and the din of knives and forks had quieted down, they began to consider possible ways for Tanner to repay his indebtedness. But Tanner refused to entertain her first suggestion.

"Absolutely not. I will not set Susan up with another man. Hank would never forgive me. In fact he'd probably kill me. Do you really want to be a widow before the wedding?"

"But I think Susan should have the chance to see other men, before she decides if Hank is who she wants," Lara argued.

"She already decided that, when she married him twelve years ago," Tanner insisted.

"They were just kids when they got married. People change."

"Those two haven't. They were always meant to be together and always will be. Instead of fixing her up with other guys, we ought to try getting her back with Hank."

"Hank doesn't deserve her."

"Sure he does."

"He cheated on her," Lara said furiously, "and don't you dare give me that bull about it just being a one-night stand. You ever try that with me, and I'll, I'll . . ."

"Careful," he cautioned, silently forbidding her to use the *D* word.

"I'll introduce you to the backside of a cast iron skillet," she finished.

To her surprise, Tanner nodded. "Fair enough, and if you should ever get confused over whose bed you're supposed to be warming, I'll let your fanny get intimately acquainted with my belt. The point is, we aren't going to let stupid mistakes ruin our marriage, and neither should the Metcalfs."

He was right, she realized. She wanted to condemn Hank's behavior as inexcusable, but there was actually very little that couldn't be excused, if you loved someone enough. That was how much she loved Tanner, and she suspected that was how much Susan loved Hank.

"Okay," she said with a gesture of surrender, "you win. We'll get them together. It shouldn't be hard. She was ready to let him move back in before I opened my big mouth."

"Whoa," Tanner warned. "I think your advice was excellent. I don't want her to take Hank back just for the kids' sake, and that's not what he wants, either. It has to be for love."

"For love," she agreed. "Any ideas?"

"Not yet, but I'm working on one. I think I'd better have a little talk with Hank tomorrow."

"Fine, I'll sound out Susan. Now what about Kelly?" Lara asked. "Who do you know that we could introduce her to?"

"I don't know," Tanner said thoughtfully. "I don't suppose there's any chance L.J. would move back to Morristown?"

"L.J.? You mean my brother? My brother and Kelly? You've got to be kidding!" Lara laughed at the very idea.

"I don't see anything so funny about it. He chased her all through his senior year in high school."

"L.J.?" Lara repeated incredulously. "L.J. and Kelly?"

"L.J. and Kelly," he reiterated firmly. "I bet he asked her out at least once a day throughout that entire year."

"But Kelly never said anything about it to me," Lara protested.

"That's not surprising. You were still in junior high at the time. Besides, she never said much to L.J., either. Except no, that is."

"But why wouldn't she go out with him?" Lara asked.

"I don't know. Kelly was just a freshman then. Maybe she wasn't allowed to date yet."

"We are talking about the same Kelly? What her parents allowed had nothing to do with what she did."

Tanner shrugged helplessly. "I don't know, Lara. You'll have to ask Kelly."

"Oh, I will. You can bet on it. The very next time I see her."

He would have bet on it, too, if there had been any takers. There was no mistaking the purposeful gleam in Lara's eye. He just wished he could be there when she cross-examined her friend.

Nobody in the Morristown High School had understood Kelly's reluctance to date the star of the football team, the son of a respected businessman. Of course, Tanner reminded himself, no one had really understood Kelly Ryan in those days. The label Rebel without a Cause had fitted her to a T.

"How did you get to be friends with her, anyway?" Tanner asked suddenly. He couldn't have imagined two teenagers more diametrically opposed, except for L.J. and Kelly, of course.

"We were both in the band."

"Ah, yes. Music, the common denominator."

"Well, it was for us, anyway. It certainly wasn't for her and her parents. Anyway, for some reason we always wound up sitting next to each other on the band bus. That's how I got to know Susan, too," she added.

"They were both two years ahead of me, but somehow I got along better with them than the kids in my own grade. I really missed them after they graduated. That's why I skipped my last year."

"You skipped your senior year?"

"Uh-huh. I was bored with school, and I was too straight for all the usual senior high jinks. My friends had already graduated, so I didn't see any point in hanging around."

"But what about your degree?"

"I never got one from high school. I was accepted as a special admission at Hendrix."

"I'm going to marry a lawyer who's a high school dropout," Tanner mumbled. "Who would have believed it?"

"It won't bother you, will it Tanner?" she asked seriously.

"That you're a dropout? Of course not."

"No, silly. I mean my being a lawyer. Having a career."

"Having an income bigger than mine, you mean? No, it doesn't bother me. If worse came to worst and we lost the farm, it's nice to know the kids won't have to go barefoot." He hesitated a moment, then turned the question on her. "Does it bother you that I'm a dirt-poor farmer?"

"No, it doesn't bother me," she replied, echoing his own sentiment. "If worse comes to worst and I'm sued for malpractice, it's nice to know the children won't starve."

He reached across the table to hold her hand. "I'm really glad you came home to Morristown."

"Me, too, Tanner. But speaking of home, I think it's time I headed to mine."

"Why?" he asked. "Just stay here. Nobody's going to mind."

"Our families would mind. I don't want our relationship to be something they're ashamed of. As long as we're discreet, nobody cares if we fool around a little, but openly living together would never do." Without waiting to discuss it further, she dashed up the stairs to get dressed.

Tanner let her go, knowing she was right. It was an old-fashioned town. That was what made it such a good place to live, the kind of place where he wanted to raise his family.

Too old-fashioned for Lara to drive home without a blouse under her jacket, he thought, as she came back downstairs in the navy-blue pinstripe and her bra.

"You are not leaving the house like that," he informed her imperiously.

"I don't have a choice," Lara argued. "You ripped my blouse."

"But that's indecent exposure!" he protested. "Weren't you the one who was just lecturing me on the need for propriety in a small town?"

"For heaven's sake, Tanner. I'm not planning to stop at Riley's or run into the market. I'll just go straight home."

"And what if you have car trouble or you're in an accident?"

"Tanner, listen to yourself!" she exclaimed. "You sound like an irate father."

"Well, damn it, what would your father think of your running around town half-naked?"

"Tanner! Oh, all right." She conceded defeat. "Give me your shirt, if it's that important."

He shook off his shirt and gave it to her, watching with hawklike eyes to make sure she buttoned every button, grumbling to himself the whole time.

"What did you say?" Lara demanded.

"I said, maybe we'll have all boys."

"Wouldn't you like a daughter?"

Tanner shook his head. "I don't think my heart could stand the strain."

"Don't worry. I'm sure you'll manage it." She gave him a quick peck and was out the door before he could pull her back and demand a proper kiss.

It actually wasn't very late, but Tanner had had a tough couple of days. He stacked their dinner dishes in the sink, then walked through the house, turning out the lights. When the house was finally settled for the night, he took himself upstairs to bed.

He smiled as his head hit the pillow. The sheets and cases didn't smell new anymore. Now they possessed an exotic perfume of Tanner and Lara. Love and passion. Tanner inhaled the heady scent, falling asleep as the visions it evoked filled his mind.

Sometime during the night, though, his thoughts began to focus on another young woman. One who stole men's hearts with her sweet smell of innocence. Their daughter was going to be a handful of trouble, he decided. But she would definitely be worth it.

11

THE NEXT FEW WEEKS were hectic for the lovers. Tanner was busy getting ready to harvest the wheat and plant the rice and soybeans. He got up early to work the fields before heading off to the auctions, searching for bargains on much-needed equipment and cheap spare parts. The bank loan finally came through on the first of March, and he had to fit the installation of the new irrigation system into his already busy schedule.

Things were just as busy for Lara. She had five new cases to deal with, in addition to the assistance she was giving Bill Harris on a criminal trial.

What free time they did have, they spent together, making wedding plans and unsuccessfully playing Cupid for their friends.

Tanner had suggested that Hank tell his wife everything, which was the advice Susan had given Tanner.

"Hell, she's already found out everything!" Hank roared back. "That's what got me into this mess in the first place."

"I mean, tell her why it happened," Tanner elaborated. "There must have been something wrong in the first place, or you wouldn't have been looking elsewhere. Tell her why you did it."

"If you think I'm going to intentionally remind her about that night, you're crazy," Hank said. "My only chance is that she'll just forget it altogether. Just try to get Lara to stall the divorce proceedings long enough."

"I can't ask Lara to do anything unethical," Tanner warned him, "but she is going to try talking to Susan."

"I'm not sure if that's a good idea," Hank said.

"Don't worry," Tanner assured him. "Lara's not against you anymore."

"Thanks, Tanner. I guess that alone is some progress."

"Cheer up, pal. Maybe the wedding will put Susan in a more forgiving frame of mind."

"Well, at least it will give me the opportunity to see her. I'm really glad you asked me to stand up for you, Tanner."

"Hey, you're the one who's going to be doing me the favor," Tanner replied.

ACROSS TOWN, Lara hoped that her fiancé was having more success than she was. Susan Metcalf had become as unmovable as a brick wall in regard to her husband. When Susan unexpectedly appeared at her office, Lara, the devil's advocate, found herself arguing the other side of the case.

"But I thought you wanted me to go through with the divorce," Susan complained.

"I never said that," Lara denied. "I said that you should consider all the possibilities."

"Well, I have."

"That's impossible, Susan. You haven't had time."

"Lara, you should have heard him when I said we should try dating again. He exploded. I'm tired of being married to a human volcano. Let him erupt on somebody else from now on."

"Oh, come on. Hank's always had that fiery temper. It never bothered you before. In fact, I remember how you used to brag about being able to defuse the explosives.

"Besides," Lara continued, "we both know that Hank is more like a firecracker than a stick of dynamite. There's a lot of noise and colorful language, but he isn't really dangerous."

"I know," her friend admitted wearily, "I'm just tired of dealing with it, Lara. It seems like I'm always the one who has to say I'm sorry. I'm the one who always has to back down. It's his turn."

She tossed her head angrily. "Do you know that when I caught him with that woman, he even had the nerve to blame it on me? It was my fault, because I didn't have enough time for him. What do you do when your husband fools around, because you're busy trying to do a good job and be a good mother?"

Lara hated it when clients asked her questions that she didn't have answers for. She hated it even more when the client was her friend. "I don't know what to tell you, Susan. If the divorce is what you want and you don't have any doubts, I'll reactivate the file. I just don't want to be the instrument used to destroy a marriage between two people who are still in love with each other."

"What makes you think Hank still loves me?" Susan demanded.

"He told us, Tanner and me. Hank came over to the farm that Saturday, just before we had the big fight."

Lara shivered as the memory of Hank on the rampage came back all too clearly. She didn't envy any woman who had to deal with that temper. Tanner's seemed incredibly mild by comparison.

"Well, why hasn't he told me that?" Susan asked. "Why can't he tell me that he loves me?"

"I don't know," Lara answered, noticing that her client hadn't denied still loving her husband. "I wish I did. Maybe I could knock some sense into him."

"Tanner owes me," Susan reminded her. "Tell him to see if he can't knock some sense into that idiot I married. If he just tries, I'll consider the debt paid in full."

"He and I will both give it our best shot," Lara promised. "In the meantime, what do you say I keep your file on hold? Okay?"

"Okay."

"Great. Now that business is out of the way, I have a favor of my own to ask you. How would you feel about being my matron of honor?"

"Matron of—? Boy, when you guys make up, you don't do it halfway, do you?"

"Well, the wedding won't be till June 15, but it is definite."

"Are you trying to give Jodi enough time to make an appearance, or are you thinking she won't come till the end of the summer?" Susan asked.

"I'm not doing either. Whether she comes back before or after the wedding, I'm not giving him up."

"Good for you!" the other woman applauded. "Oh, Lara, I am so happy for you."

"Does that mean you'll be the matron of honor?"

"By June, I might be a maid again, but either way I'd love to stand up with you," Susan assured her.

Later that afternoon, Lara swung by the band room at the high school to pin down her first choice for bridesmaid. She stood in the back, reliving old memories as Kelly concluded her last class for the day.

She couldn't help but smile as she found herself keeping tempo right along with the one hundred plus students in the room. It pleased her that Kelly's first trumpet was a girl. She wondered if that child's parents had thought the instrument as unfeminine a choice as Lara's had.

Her minor rebellion had been nothing compared to Kelly's, though. Lara wondered how many of these students would have recognized their diligent, bespectacled conductor as the wild-haired, foulmouthed girl she had once known.

The last bell rang, and the clamor and jostling of the students quickly brought Lara back to the present. She waited patiently as Kelly finished giving some practice tips to her first-chair flute. It occurred to her as she eavesdropped that she was seeing an entirely new side of her friend.

"Who would have guessed Kelly Ryan would have ever ended up as an authority figure?" Lara asked out loud, when the flutist ran off to catch her bus.

"Is that what I am?" Kelly cried. "Quick, where do I resign?"

"Yes, that's what you are, and you know perfectly well you won't resign until you are too deaf to hear the sharps where there shouldn't be any."

The band director wrinkled her freckled nose in disgust. "Does it show that much?"

"Yes," Lara said emphatically.

"Mmm, I'll have to work on that. If the school board realizes that I'm really doing this just for love, they'll never give me a raise."

"Yes, they will," Lara promised. "Besides, you can't fool all those kids or their parents. You've done a great job with the music program since you've been here, and it won't go unrewarded."

"I always knew they put you in the wrong class," Kelly told her and laughed. "You are a born cheerleader."

"Thanks a lot. I throw compliments at your feet and all I get is insults."

"You're right, you didn't deserve that. I take it back."

"Thank you, I might let you be in the wedding, after all."

"Did you say wedding?" When Lara nodded happily, Kelly shouted with joy. "All right! Oh, wow! I'm so happy for you guys. I knew Tanner was the guy for you that night at the Jube. Oh, and when he told Susan and me how much he loved you, we both started crying."

"He does say the most romantic things, doesn't he?" Lara asked dreamily.

"Mmm. And to think I might have snagged him myself, if you hadn't shown up."

"Kelly!"

"Oh, all right. I won't hold it against you. But Tanner owes me, and I want to be repaid in kind. One Cupid's arrow deserves another."

"Don't worry," Lara assured her. "We're both working on it."

"Great. Maybe I won't die an old maid, after all."

"From what I hear, if you do, it won't be the fault of the male population. You aren't still single because of a lack of proposals," Lara pointed out.

"That might have been true once," Kelly lamented, "but I received all those offers when I still had the time to be choosy. Now I'm reaching the age of despair, and all those possibilities have gone off and married someone else. And speaking of marriage," she said, deftly shifting the subject back to Lara, "when is yours going to be?"

"June 15."

"I see," Kelly drawled. "You've decided to give Jodi a fair chance, but you aren't going to clear the field for her entirely."

"That has nothing to do with it," Lara denied for the second time that day.

"Sure," her friend said. "Why don't you pull the other leg? That one's a little worn out."

"I just want time to plan a nice wedding," Lara insisted. "The quickie variety certainly didn't bring me any luck last time."

"It's the person you're marrying who matters," Kelly lectured her. "Not the wedding. Anyone with the degrees you have hanging on your office wall should know that."

"I know," Lara admitted, "but this time I want to do everything right and give us the best start possible. That includes a traditional wedding with the works, and that takes time to arrange."

"And if it just happens to give Jodi time to appear and assure you that it really is over between her and Tanner, that's just an added bonus," Kelly guessed.

"Right," Lara said.

"That's what I thought."

"Honestly, Kelly, you can be so infuriating sometimes. I don't know why I want you to be my bridesmaid."

"Your bridesmaid! Really? Oh, Lara, I would love to!" Kelly exclaimed. But her excitement vanished as quickly as it had appeared. "Wait a second. You said traditional. That means in a church, doesn't it?"

"Relax," Lara told her, well aware of her friend's church phobia. "Tanner and I decided to hold it in the rose garden out at the farm. We both consider ourselves part of the multidenominational set. This way we won't offend any of our churches by having to choose one of them."

"Thank goodness," Kelly said. "I would have hated to have missed the ceremony. Especially since I'm going to be part of it."

"I can count on you then?" Lara asked.

"Definitely. I wouldn't miss this for the world. You should let Tanner write the vows. Something beautiful and romantic."

"You know, that's not a bad idea. I'm not so fond of that obey line myself. Thanks for the suggestion, Kelly."

"You're welcome. I can help you plan the music, too? An organ's out of the question, if you're getting married in a garden."

"Mmm, I hadn't thought about that."

"Well, you don't have to. I'll draw up a list of suggestions for you, and you can just pick the one that sounds best."

"You're a godsend, Kelly. Tanner and I are going to owe you a lot more than a prospective husband at this rate."

"Don't worry. A man will do just fine." She paused. "By the way, who's going to stand up with Tanner?"

Lara cleared her throat uncomfortably. "Well, he insists on Hank being his best man."

"Uh-oh. Dare I guess that you have asked Susan to be the matron of honor?" At Lara's nod, Kelly whistled sharply. "Did you tell her who would be escorting her down the aisle?"

"No. I decided to wait till we've got your dresses. She wouldn't dare back out on me then."

Kelly pretended shock. "Lara, I never knew you could play so dirty. Maybe there's hope for you, after all." Her spirited grin faded suddenly as another thought struck her. "Wait a minute. Who's going to be my escort?"

Lara smiled this time. This revelation might prove to be very interesting. "Tanner is going to ask Little John."

For the first time in Lara's memory, Kelly appeared completely dumbfounded. "Not your brother? Not that Little John? Not L.J., the great football hero? Not Johnnie?"

Johnnie? Lara had never heard anyone call her big brother Johnnie before. So Tanner hadn't been mistaken, after all. There had been something between the rebel and the hero. How very interesting.

"Lara, didn't you hear me? I asked you if Tanner meant Little John, as in your big brother."

"Well, of course he meant my Little John," she answered. "I didn't know there was any other."

"That's what I was afraid of," Kelly said. "Lara, maybe you should just let me be the music director for the ceremonies. One attendant is more than enough for a garden wedding."

"Oh, no!" Lara vetoed the suggestion loudly. "You already promised, and I'm going to hold you to it. Are you free to go shopping this weekend? We might as well start looking at dresses now."

"I guess so," Kelly said with a noticeable lack of enthusiasm.

"Terrific. We'll drive to Memphis and make a day of it. Just the three of us. It'll be a blast."

THE CHORUS OF "Going to the Chapel" rang out joyously and repeatedly from the Mercedes as Lara drove to the farm. She couldn't remember the rest of the song, but the words she did recall seemed more than adequate for the occasion.

The lyrics faded into a soft humming as Lara got out of the car and went in search of her husband-to-be. She finally located him in the shed, underneath his tractor.

"Hi!" she called to him. "Is it quitting time yet?"

Tanner quickly slid out from under his big, blue monster to greet her. His excitement at seeing her was quashed when Lara jumped back from his welcoming arms.

"What's wrong?" he asked in concern, stepping forward to narrow the space between them.

"Nothing, except you are covered with oil, and I'm still wearing a good suit. Let's save the hugs and kisses till later, okay?"

Tanner glanced down at his grease-covered hands and coveralls. "Okay, on the hug, but I think it's safe to give me a kiss," he said.

Lara quirked an eyebrow, taking note of the streaks on his cheeks and forehead. "Obviously you haven't looked in a mirror lately."

He immediately reached up to wipe his face, forgetting about his even greasier hands, swearing profusely when he realized he had only made matters worse. Lara was no help at all, doubled over with laughter as she was.

"Think it's pretty funny, do you? Let's see who's laughing when you're the one wearing the grease-paint," Tanner suggested. He made a swipe at her with one grimy paw, but Lara managed to dodge him at the last second.

"No, Tanner. Stop. I'll quit laughing, I promise."

"What's the matter?" he teased. "Is the lady lawyer afraid to get her hands dirty?"

"It isn't my hands I'm worried about," she said, slipping around to the other side of the tractor. She had meant to put a barrier between them, but her plan backfired on her. Instead of staying on the other side, where he belonged, Tanner dropped to the ground and crawled beneath the machine. He almost had one delicate ankle in his clutches when Lara caught on.

She jumped back quickly, just barely managing to elude his grasp.

But Tanner was in such a hurry to make a second attempt that he raised his head before it had cleared the tractor's underbelly.

Lara cringed as she heard the awful thwack of skull clashing with metal. "Oh, Tanner, are you all right?" She forgot all about her expensive suit and dropped to the ground.

Tanner moaned loudly, covering the back of his head with his hands.

Grabbing two fistfuls of coverall, Lara hauled him out from under the machine, jabbering questions of concern without ever giving him a chance to answer. "Honey, are you all right? Say something. Are you okay? Oh, please tell me you're okay."

Rolling him over as gently as she could, she brought his head to rest in her lap and dabbed the grease away from his eyes with a soiled bandanna she pulled from his pocket. "Can you hear me? Darling, please say something."

One eyelid finally fluttered open, revealing a tawny-golden eye, bright with barely contained mirth. "Gotcha."

"Oh, you rat!" Lara lurched to her feet, letting Tanner's head fall to the floor with another painful thwack.

"Ouch!" he hollered. "That hurt!"

"It serves you right for letting me think you were injured."

"I am injured now, believe me." Tanner groaned, wincing as he touched a tender spot on his head.

"Good," Lara said, then spoiled the effect as she grabbed his elbow and helped him to his feet. "Come on, I'll fix you an ice pack."

"No, thanks," Tanner said. "You'll probably throw it at me or slip it down my back."

"Don't be silly," she told him, leading him into the kitchen. She might have done either and more, but it wouldn't be any fun if he was expecting it.

She chose, instead, to relate her conversations with Susan and Kelly, giving him a full report on Project Cupid. He winced as she told him about Susan, but not from the pain in his head. How were they ever going to get those two back together?

And Kelly's case wasn't going to be any easier. It was more than a little tricky to pair up two people who had the width of the entire state of Arkansas separating them.

"But we've already found a way to get them together," Lara pointed out. "The wedding. Susan and Hank and Kelly and Little John will have to see each other then. And at the rehearsal dinner and the reception also."

"That's true," Tanner agreed, "but that's still three and a half months away. Unless you want to move the wedding up?" he suggested hopefully.

"Nice try," Lara told him, "but the wedding is fine, right where it is. We just need to think of something to do in the meantime to help set them up."

"Any suggestions?" he asked.

"Well, I did have one thought. I know you don't want to fix Susan up with anyone who might stand in Hank's way, but what would you say to fixing her up with someone who wouldn't be any competition?"

Tanner frowned. "I'm not sure I follow you."

"Susan has decided that she deserves better than Hank. But what if we show her that Hank's the pick of the litter?"

"You mean deliberately set her up with guys we know she couldn't possibly like?" Tanner asked.

"Yep."

"Lara Jamison, I am truly shocked. Who would have ever thought you were capable of something so sneaky?"

She grinned. "Think it would work?"

"Well, I guess it wouldn't hurt. For that matter, we might as well try it with Kelly, too. If she realizes her options are limited, maybe she'll think twice before she says no to L.J. again."

"Fair enough," Lara agreed.

The two began to compile a selection of undesirables for their friends, coming up with a surprisingly long list. In fact, the more men they considered, the more confident they became that Hank and L.J. were the only possible choices for their two friends.

"What about Hank and L.J.?" Lara suddenly asked. "Shouldn't we be working on them, too?"

"Why?" Tanner asked. "They're already sold on the girls."

"Well, I know Hank is sold on Susan, but what makes you so sure about L.J.?"

"You should have heard him, when I told him who he'd be escorting down the aisle. I had the feeling that

I'm not the only one who wishes the wedding were tomorrow."

Lara kissed him soundly. "Don't worry. It'll be here soon enough."

12

ON THE LAST DAY of April Tanner walked proudly through one hundred acres of waist-high grain, ripe heads rippling in the wind. *Yes, Lara*, he thought, *farmers do believe in fate.* He was certainly grateful for the quirk that had allowed the March hailstorm, which had flattened Midwestern fields, to subside into blessed, drenching rains by the time they reached the Arkansas delta.

Now the wet, gray skies had vanished, replaced by bright, warm sunshine. The wheat had grown tall, changing in color from spring green to a rich, harvest gold. The ground was dry. Tomorrow, May 1, he would begin the winter harvest and make room for the soybeans that followed the wheat in the growing cycle.

Two hundred acres that had lain dormant through the past six months had already been planted in rice; it now covered the ground with a good, two-inch stand. Soon it would be time to put on the first flood. If the weather held, and he prayed for that every day, this would be his best year ever.

Tanner's rose garden had also prospered, his vision becoming a reality as the climbers began to mount the arbor and new leaves adorned the thorny limbs. By June 1, he predicted the white paint would barely be visible beneath a green cloak studded with multicolored buds and blossoms.

The rose garden should be hitting its peak just in time for the wedding, he decided. It was indeed a beautiful world, and the day he had feared would never arrive was approaching faster than he had dreamed possible.

LARA SAT at her desk, turning the letter over and over. He must have heard about the wedding, she realized. She hadn't sent him a wedding invitation, but she had told friends in Houston, and one of them must have told her ex-husband. Why else would he write? Kevin never wrote letters.

She inserted the tip of the steel blade, then quickly pushed the letter opener through the flap and jerked it up before she could change her mind. Then she removed the pages, holding them lightly with just the tips of her fingers, and began to read:

Dear Lara,

I know you must be surprised to hear from me. I have to admit I am a little surprised at myself for writing. But I've been thinking of you a great deal lately.

The azaleas you planted are in full bloom now. They really make the house look beautiful. Every time I look at them, I think of you, puttering around in those awful gardening clothes, and I wonder all over again how someone could look so lovely with sunburned cheeks and a smudge of dirt on her nose. But you did look lovely. So very lovely.

Since you left, I've often wondered if the sophisticated city woman I knew could really go back to being a small-town girl. I suppose the azaleas should have answered that question. I realize now that a large part of you had always remained back in that little city you are so proud of.

Yesterday I heard that you were getting married to one of your locals. If it's true, I hope that you'll be happy. And I hope that your new husband will have more sense than your old one.

Somehow I've held on to this dream of you and me growing old together, sitting on a veranda, looking out over the ocean, watching the sun set beyond the waves. I suppose I'll have to let go of that now.

I miss you, Lara. I am only sorry it took me so long to realize how much. If things don't work out there, if you are ever in need of anything, call me. Maybe what we had wasn't the happily ever after, but it was very special.

Love always,
Kevin

Carefully she refolded the letter and replaced it in the envelope, aware that her hands were trembling only slightly. She closed her eyes, fluttering her lashes to clear the misty tears that had gathered. Inside she felt a faint stirring, a memory warming.

IT HAD BEEN a long day. Tanner was hot and tired, and worried about that clanging noise he heard the combine make on the last sweep. The winter harvest was almost complete, and, *if* Big Blue held up, he might be able to finish before the sun went down.

She caught him off guard. For the first time in seven years, his senses had failed to warn him of her presence. He'd always been able to feel her coming when she was still miles down the road, but this time he hadn't realized it until she was standing almost directly behind him.

"I'm back," she said.

The words blew shivers down his spine. Slowly he turned around, his mind a complete blank. He hadn't prepared a speech this time. He had no idea what to say.

"Hello, Jodi. I'm surprised to see you."

"I said I'd be back," she reminded him. "I even sent a postcard."

"So you did," he agreed. "I guess I just expected you to change your mind. Weren't there any new places beckoning? Somewhere you hadn't been yet? Somewhere best seen in the summer?"

"There are many such places," she answered. "We can see them together."

"No," he said firmly, "I don't think so."

In her hand Jodi twisted a stem of wheat, shredding the head into a million tiny pieces that fell from her fingers and flew off on the wind. "I'll stay here with you, then. We can spend the summer together, like we always do."

"You mean like we used to do," he corrected. "Those days are over, Jodi."

"They don't have to be." She stepped closer, but didn't touch him. Jodi never touched him first.

"Yes, they do," Tanner said. "I'm not looking for a summer romance anymore."

"I'll stay this time," she whispered, then repeated her words, louder. "Do you hear me, Tanner? I'll stay this time. I promise."

"Jodi, stop it." He grabbed her by the shoulders, shaking her without intending to. "You don't mean it. You couldn't stay here any more than I can leave. We're different, you and I. We are two different kinds of people."

"But we love each other." At last Jodi stretched out her own arms.

Tanner slid his hands down from her shoulders to her wrists, pulling her hands away from his body. "No, we don't. What we shared was simple companionship, uncomplicated and undemanding. Love is much more than that."

"You've found someone else, haven't you?" she asked.

Tanner closed his eyes, not wanting to see her pain, not wanting to hurt her. "That doesn't matter. It's been over for us for a long time, Jodi."

"Is she pretty?"

Tanner felt his jaw clench with frustration. "This has nothing to do with anyone else," he said firmly.

"I don't believe you."

He looked up at the sky, hoping irrationally that fate would somehow provide an answer as generously as it had provided the rain. Unfortunately, this time he was on his own. There was only one thing he knew how to do. It was the only thing that had seemed to work for him lately.

Lara wrote back.

Dear Kevin

I just received your letter, and I can't tell you how deeply it touched me.

There were times after our divorce when I foolishly wished we'd never met, never married. Now I realize how valuable that part of my life is, and I wouldn't wish it away for anything in the world.

What we had was special, and I'm glad that you will also remember it well. I would hate to think that the "happily" part had to go to waste, simply because we won't be able to share the "ever after."

It is true. I am getting married. Tanner is a wonderful man, and he shares my hopes and dreams for the future. This time I truly believe it will be forever.

But please, don't give up your own dream. Somewhere out there is a woman who would love to sit on that veranda and share those sunsets with you. I wish you all the luck in the world at finding her.

Don't hesitate to let me know if there is ever anything I can do to help.

Love always,
Lara

"Come on," Tanner said, grabbing Jodi's arm and pulling her along beside him. "There's something I want to show you." He led her through the field and around the house, not pausing until they had reached the rose garden.

When he stopped abruptly and released her, Jodi walked toward the arbor, which was already partially covered with rose branches and a few, tiny buds. "It's beautiful," she told him. "But why did you rebuild it?"

"To atone for my sins."

"I don't understand."

"It was a hard winter for me, Jodi. I did a lot of things I wasn't proud of."

"Tanner, I don't know what you're talking about. I'm not sure I want to."

"But it's important. I tried to destroy you. In a way, I did. I destroyed the Jodi I was trying to create, the false image I believed I could keep and mold into the woman I wanted."

He folded his arms across his chest, staring off into the distance, as if somewhere out there he could still see the bonfire burning.

"I came out here in a rage one night, dragging every reminder of you and all that you could never be, and tossed it into a pile. Then I burned it. All of it. Everything you ever gave me, virtually everything of mine you ever touched."

He saw Jodi's face grow ashen, the sky-blue eyes widening into huge circles in shock.

"The next day, I took the ashes and added them to this earth." His hands swept out to indicate the garden. "Then I replanted the roses and rebuilt the arbor."

"This is for me, then?" she asked. "For my forgiveness?"

"No, Jodi, not for you. I did all this so I could forgive myself, and so I could prove to the woman I do love that I was over the past and was ready to commit to a future with her."

"So there is someone else?" Her voice trembled as she spoke. The familiar, red pack slid to the ground as she reached out to grab the arbor's railing for support.

"Jodi, I don't want to hurt you, but I'm going to be as honest with you as I know how to be."

She stepped inside the arbor and began to walk around, one hand idly trailing across the hammock. "Go on, I'm listening."

"There is someone else. I love her very much, just as she is. In a few weeks we're going to be married. Right here in this garden. She and I are right for each other, Jodi. We share dreams and values, but more than that, we share a love that is stronger and deeper than I knew love could be."

"But I thought you loved me."

"I care for you, Jodi. I want you to be happy, and I hope that you will find someone who is as perfect for you as Lara and I are for each other. But you'll never find him until you let go of the illusion. That's what we are, Jodi. An illusion."

"No. No, we were more than that," she protested. "I know we were. And we could still be."

"Jodi, listen to me," he pleaded. "You've walked through deserts. You know the danger of being confused by a mirage. You see water because it's what you want to see, but if you stop when you see the illusion, you'll die. You have to keep searching until you find the true oasis, or the desert will beat you."

She shook her head violently. "No, no, no."

He stepped forward but stayed on the outside of the arbor. His voice deepened and grew stronger. "Listen to me, Jodi. Life is like that desert. You and I stopped searching too soon. We settled for a mirage, because it was easier than continuing to search for the real thing. But that's cheating, babe. And you don't want to be cheated."

Tanner reached out and grabbed her hands, pulling her out of the rose-covered shelter. "This isn't the place for you, Jodi. I'm not the man for you. But the right man and the right place are out there somewhere, if you'll just keep searching."

When he would have released his grip, she held on, threading her fingers through his to tighten her hold. "Tell me the difference then, Tanner. If what we had wasn't real, then tell me how to recognize what is, because it sure had me fooled."

"It had me fooled for a long time, too, Jodi. I don't deny that." Tanner lifted his hands, but didn't try to pull them away when she refused to release his fingers. "I suppose a man who had never tasted water might be fooled into drinking sand, but once he's tasted just a single drop of rain, he'll never make that mistake again."

He brought their left and right hands together between them, then pried her fingers away from his and pressed her palms together. Separating their bodies, as he was trying to separate their lives.

"That's all I can tell you, Jodi. Once you have found that true love, you'll recognize him, and you'll never confuse him with anyone else again. I can't describe how, any more than I can describe the taste of a drop of rain. But after you've experienced it for yourself, it will be just as clear as the difference between sand and water."

He lifted his hand to the curve of her neck and pulled out the chain that bore the inscribed medallion. "We should have known the day I gave you this that we weren't meant for each other. You don't need someone to wait for you, Jodi, someone who asks you to come back. You need someone who'll walk beside you."

Jodi stared at his face for a long moment before she spoke. "I hope she appreciates what she's getting," she said at last.

Tanner shook his head slowly. "I wish I could make you appreciate what it is I have found."

"I do appreciate it, but you'll have to forgive me if I don't celebrate with you." She bent down and grasped her pack, slinging it onto her back.

"Jodi, wait. Don't go like this."

"Why not? This isn't the place for me. You just said so yourself."

"I'll worry about you."

She gave him a sad, knowing smile. "You always worry too much, Tanner, but you don't have to worry about me anymore. At least now I know what it is I'm looking for."

He would still worry. "Jodi, if you ever need anything, if you ever need help or even just a place to stay, to rest for a while. . . ."

"Sure," she said, "I'll let you know."

"Damn it, Jodi, I do care."

"I know." This time her words sounded sincere. "It was pretty good for a mirage, don't you think?"

"Very good."

She gave him a light kiss on the cheek and then turned away, but only managed a few steps before he brought her to a halt. He placed a thin, silver coin in her palm.

"For a phone call?"

"Or a postcard," he suggested. "When you find the real thing."

Jodi flipped the quarter in her palm. It landed heads up. She tucked it into her pocket and set off again.

"Promise you will let me know," he called after her.

She turned around, still walking backward, and the wind carried her words to him. "I promise."

SHE HAD JUST dropped the letter to Kevin into the mailbox when the first messenger appeared.

"Lara, thank goodness, I found you!" Susan Metcalf climbed out of her illegally parked car and hurried toward her.

"Is something wrong?" she asked, alarmed by her friend's fluster.

"That depends on how you look at it, I guess. Jodi's back. She is here in Morristown, Lara. I saw her on my way in from an interview. She was heading down Highway One toward the farm."

"You're sure it was her?"

"Positive." Susan crossed her heart and then held her hand up to heaven.

Lara sighed. "Well, at least we'll be able to get that out of the way before the wedding."

Her calm acceptance of the news stunned Susan. "Is that all you're going to say? Aren't you worried?"

"Why should I be?" Lara shrugged. "Aren't you the one who convinced me that Tanner didn't love Jodi anymore?"

"Well, yes, but . . ."

"But you aren't sure now? Is that it?"

"No, no. I am sure he loves you, but . . ."

Lara laughed much easier than she would have thought possible a few weeks ago. The long engagement had been a wonderful idea. Her faith in Tanner had grown by leaps and bounds, as had her love for him. She knew Jodi's appearance wasn't a threat to her, any more than Kevin's letter had been a threat to Tanner.

"What do you want me to do, Susan? Dash out there? Try to head her off at the pass?"

"Well, yes," Susan admitted. "Something like that."

Lara shook her head. "Sorry. This is out of my territory. Tanner will take care of Jodi, and I trust him to do it in the best possible way."

Susan studied her friend for a long, silent moment. "You've changed," she said finally. "Just a few weeks ago you were a bundle of nerves, because you were afraid he wasn't over Jodi."

"Time has a way of making you see things clearly," Lara told her friend. "These past months have shown me how much Tanner loves me, and how much I love him. And trust him. Jodi doesn't worry me anymore."

"I'm envious," Susan confessed. "I wish I could learn to trust Hank like that again."

"Maybe you will in time. Come on. Park your car legally, and let's go over to Riley's for some coffee."

They had just sat down at their usual booth when Kelly came dashing in. "Lara, you'll never guess who I just saw!"

Susan exchanged a knowing smile with Lara. "Sorry, Kelly. I already beat you to the scoop."

"But if you know, why are you still sitting here? Let's go!"

"Go where?" Lara asked her.

"The farm, of course. That must be where she was headed."

"Sit down, Kelly," Susan said.

"But . . ."

"Sit down. Lara is going to let Tanner handle it, and I am sure that he doesn't need an audience. It will be hard enough for Jodi, as it is."

Kelly slid into the booth and stared at them in disbelief. "Are you two getting senile or something? Have you forgotten who Jodi is?"

"I haven't forgotten, and you're older than I am, so watch it." Lara finished her cup of coffee and ordered another, ignoring Kelly's agitation.

"I can't believe you can just sit here so calmly, while some other woman tries to steal your man."

"Jodi isn't trying to steal him," Lara explained. "She's come back to see if there is still a chance for them. Tanner will tell her there isn't, and she'll be on her way again."

"You really think it will be that easy?" Kelly inquired, expressing her doubt.

"I never said anything about easy. I'm sure it will be very difficult for both of them. But I do think it is that simple."

"Leave her alone," Susan ordered. "She's right."

Kelly obviously still had her doubts, but she settled back in her seat and requested a cup for herself. "Maybe she is. Who am I to argue with success? Lara is certainly doing better than we are when it comes to love."

"Which reminds me," Susan interrupted, turning toward her would-be Cupid. "Where are you and Tanner getting these men you've been fixing us up with, the zoo? I've never met such a mass of morons."

Lara sputtered into her coffee, pretending to choke in order to cover up her giggling. "Sorry, girls, but it looks like you were right. There is a severe shortage of decent men out there."

"Well, I agree with Susan. If you can't find something better than what you've been sending, don't send anyone at all," Kelly said.

"Okay, if that's the way you all feel about it," Lara replied, surrendering easily. "Tanner and I were just trying to do you a favor."

"You mean you were trying to return a favor," Susan corrected. "And don't think for a minute those barbarians you've paired us up with even the score. Kelly and I will just have to think of another way for you to repay us."

Lara shook her head sadly. "Some people are so hard to please."

Suddenly the door of the diner was flung open with force. They all turned to stare as Hank Metcalf came charging through, making a beeline for their table.

He came to an abrupt stop beside the table, tugging off the fishing hat he had been wearing. He twisted the cap in his hands, giving each of the women a quick bow of his head as he said their names. "Kelly. Lara." A brief pause. "Susan."

"Hello, Hank." Lara smiled at him, trying to ignore the hostility that was being generated by her table companions. "What brings you here?"

"I, uh, I just thought you might like to know—"

"If you're referring to the fact that Jodi's back, we've already told her. Thank you very much. You may go now." Kelly dismissed him. Susan just glared at him quietly.

They saw Hank give Kelly his most effective mean look, then turn his attention back to Lara.

"She's not back," he informed her. "She's already gone. I saw her walking away from the farm, heading mostly south. Maybe a little to the east. I just thought you might like to know."

"Thanks, Hank. I appreciate it." Lara took one last sip of coffee and then eased herself out of the booth. "If you all will excuse me, I think I'll go see how Tanner fared. See you later."

SHE FOUND HIM swinging in the hammock. He smiled and opened his arms to her. Lara sank into his embrace without hesitation.

"Jodi came back," he said quietly.

"I know."

He arched his eyebrows in surprise.

"The communications network," she explained. "Susan, Kelly and Hank all saw her walking down Route One and sounded the alarm."

He wasn't surprised to hear that. "I wish someone had alerted me," he complained. "She caught me completely off guard. I really didn't think she would come."

Lara gave him her Mona Lisa smile.

"I know, she told me she would and you told me she would, so it's my own fault for not believing you."

Lara reached out and gently smoothed the corners of his mouth, stroking away the frown that marred his handsome face. "What happened? Did you tell her about us?"

Tanner nodded. "Yes, I told her and I tried to explain, but it wasn't easy. I'm not sure if she really understood what I was trying to say."

"And what was that?" Lara asked him.

"That whatever she and I had wasn't the real thing. That someday she would find the person who was right for her, and she would realize what we both had been missing." The left corner of his mouth twitched wryly. "I don't think she bought it."

"She will in time. Remember all the stages you had to work through. She has to work through them, too. It may take a while, but someday she'll understand."

"I know," he said. "I just wish I could have made it easier."

Lara snuggled against his side, closing her eyes, smiling contentedly when she felt him rest his chin on the top of her head. One strong hand caressed her back.

"I got a letter from Kevin today."

The hand stopped for a moment, then began to circle again. "What did he say?"

"That he had heard I was getting married, that he wished me the best. That if I ever needed anything, he'd be there."

Tanner lifted his chin for a moment, his body tense. "Do you think he wants you back?"

"No. I think he meant exactly what he said."

"Are you going to write him?"

"I already have." She moved her head, nuzzling toward his chin again. "I told him that I was very happy and that someday I hoped he found someone else, too."

He tightened his arms around her, pulling her closer. She pressed a soft kiss against his chest, just above his heart. They both relaxed and let the security of their love lull them to sleep.

The wind began to stir as darkness fell and the earth let go of the warmth it had collected throughout the day from the sun. The hammock rocked gently in the breeze and the lovers lay quietly together.

ON JUNE 15th a man sat on a veranda along the Gulf Coast, waiting for sunset, wishing he wasn't alone.

A little to the east of him, a red pack bobbed along the coastline in the rhythm of a tireless traveler, continuously putting one foot in front of the other as she tried to discover the difference between sand and water.

In Morristown, Arkansas, the weather was perfect. The arbor stood covered with roses, and the hammock had been temporarily displaced. The matron of honor tried diligently to ignore the best man, and the bridesmaid wondered what she should do with the impossible groomsman.

The bride and groom were oblivious to all but each other. They repeated no vows, choosing instead to speak straight from their hearts.

"Lara Jamison, you are my whole world. The sun that warms me, the rain that nourishes me, the moon that dares me to dream. Without you I would live in darkness on a barren planet, with no desire and no purpose. If you will give me your love, I promise to care for it always, to nurture it through tender moments and harsh times, and I will return it tenfold."

"You have my love, Tanner McNeil, and together we will plant the seeds, protect them from harm and reap the harvest when our work is done. All I ask is that you return my love in kind, and I shall stay by your side and love you through all time and for all seasons."

COMING NEXT MONTH

#313 TO BUY A GROOM Rita Clay Estrada

One million dollars was the price Sable LaCroix paid Joe Lombardi to marry her. He needed money to finish building his Texas racetrack—she needed a husband to retain custody of her son. It was the perfect business arrangement on paper... but it didn't take into account their very human needs and desires.

#314 JUST JAKE Shirley Larson

Ambitious Alexandra Holden would make a killing selling her property in the Florida Keys—if she could evict Dr. Jake Hustead. But the sexy doctor proved extremely stubborn—and resourceful. He started his own campaign to change Alex's mind... with unexpected results.

#315 ONE MORE CHANCE Ruth Jean Dale

Real estate agent Juliana Robinson wasn't about to let Ben Ware thwart a deal that would bring a hefty commission. But when Ben saved her life, she was forced to look at him in a new light. She had finally found something more important than making money, but could she ever convince Ben she'd really changed?

#316 DARK SECRETS Glenda Sanders EDITOR'S CHOICE

The screams Vanessa Wiggins heard coming from her backyard were not the result of an overactive imagination—as the local sheriff seemed to think. She believed something was terribly wrong, and thankfully, so did her neighbor Taylor Stephenson. She was going to need his comfort and strength as the terrible truth began to unfold....

GLENDA SANDERS
Dark Secrets

When Vanessa Wiggins reported screams
coming from her backyard, the sheriff
convinced her no one had been murdered; no
body had been found. But Vanessa was
convinced something was terribly wrong, and
only her neighbor, Taylor Stephenson, took
her claims seriously. And then the ghost
appeared. . . .

Bestselling Temptation author Glenda Sanders
weaves the unspeakable terrors of the past
with one of today's best love stories in a special
Editor's Choice selection. But a word of
warning—don't read DARK SECRETS alone at
night. Have someone you love close by!

Coming in September 1990.

Harlequin Superromance®

THE LIVING WEST

Where men and women must be strong in both body
and spirit; where the lessons of the past must be fully
absorbed before the present can be understood; where
the dramas of everyday lives are played out against a
panoramic setting of sun, red earth, mountain and
endless sky....

Harlequin Superromance is proud to present this
powerful new trilogy by Suzanne Ellison, a veteran
Superromance writer who has long possessed a
passion for the West. Meet Joe Henderson, whose past
haunts him—and his romance with Mandy Larkin;
Tess Hamilton, who isn't sure she can make a life with
modern-day pioneer Brady Trent, though she loves
him desperately; and Clay Gann, who thinks the
cultured Roberta Wheeler isn't quite woman enough
to make it in the rugged West....

Please join us for HEART OF THE WEST (September
1990), SOUL OF THE WEST (October 1990) and
SPIRIT OF THE WEST (November 1990) and see the
West come alive!

SR-LW-420-1

COMING SOON...

For years Harlequin and Silhouette novels
have been taking readers places—but only in
their imaginations.

This fall look for PASSPORT TO ROMANCE,
a promotion that could take you around the
corner or around the world!

Watch for it in September!

★